# A Final Exam for a Spy . . .

Olga's enraged "father" and a friend burst into the room. Olga crawled from beneath Sir Edmund and began screaming that he had forced her, raped her.

The men pulled Sir Edmund from the bed and beat him. He begged them to stop hitting him, begged Olga to tell them the truth, that it was she who had seduced him.

Olga, still nude, was impassive, disinterested.

Suddenly, it was over.

"Marvelous! You have passed your final test, Olga Siskova," Sir Edmund said in perfect Russian. "Allow me to introduce myself. I am Major Smislov, KGB!"

# NICK CARTER IS IT!

"Nick Carter out-Bonds James Bond."
—*Buffalo Evening News*

"Nick Carter is America's #1 espionage agent."
—*Variety*

"Nick Carter is razor-sharp suspense."
—*King Features*

"Nick Carter has attracted an army of addicted readers . . . the books are fast, have plenty of action and just the right degree of sex . . . Nick Carter is the American James Bond, suave, sophisticated, a killer with both the ladies and the enemy."
—*The New York Times*

# FROM THE NICK CARTER
# KILLMASTER SERIES

# THE DEADLY DIVA
# KILL MASTER
# NICK CARTER

JOVE BOOKS, NEW YORK

KILLMASTER #245: THE DEADLY DIVA

A Jove book / published by arrangement with
The Condé Nast Publications, Inc.

PRINTING HISTORY
Jove edition / January 1989

ISBN: 0-515-09874-4

Jove Books are published by The Berkley Publishing Group,
200 Madison Avenue, New York, New York 10016.
The name "JOVE" and the "J" logo
are trademarks belonging to Jove Publications, Inc.

PRINTED IN THE UNITED STATES OF AMERICA

10  9  8  7  6  5  4  3  2  1

*Dedicated to the men of the
Secret Services of the
United States of America*

# ONE

The Château d'Ormanz was one of the showplaces of the Côte d'Azur. It stood alone on the top of a hill above Cannes, commanding a view of the entire sweep of sea between the Esterel hills to the west and the Maritime Alps to the east.

It had been built at the turn of the century by the aging Eugene Ormanz, who had made fortunes first in slavery and then in French railroads.

For eighty years, the place had stayed in the family. Then it and the family fortune had fallen into the hands of old Eugene's last surviving heir, his great-grandson, Palo.

Palo Ormanz loved good food, strong drink, airplanes, expensive cars, beautiful women, and gambling. He received his fortune at twenty-one. By the age of forty-one, he had gone through all of it but the château.

On his forty-second birthday, Palo had stood at the front window of the master suite and gazed out at the blue line of Corsica barely visible to the southeast.

Nearby, on a table, lay the deed to the château, a pen, and an American automatic .45.

Palo saluted the coastline with a glass of brandy, picked

1

up the pen, and signed the deed of sale.

Then he picked up the .45, put the barrel in his mouth, and blew the back of his head off.

The new owner of the Château d'Ormanz was one of Palo's many lovers. It was she who found him two hours later.

Within one week she had taken possession and had the master suite completely redone. Gone were the gaudy reds and yellows and the opulent velvets. Now it resembled a room from a Chekhov play, down to snow scenes of Moscow and the frozen steppes on the walls, and a giant bronze samovar in the corner. The piano, a huge affair, was covered with an antique lace shawl and rows of silver-framed photographs.

The owner now stood at the same window where Palo had once stood. She also drank brandy, and she was also contemplating the length of her life.

Three stories below, the lights of a Mercedes sedan moved slowly down the long, winding drive. In the Mercedes was the woman's maid, Mrs. Kranz, and her gardener, Alfred. It was a biweekly ritual. On their evening off, Alfred always took Mrs. Kranz to dinner in one of the little cafés in Cannes.

On this particular evening, Alfred's old Fiat wasn't running properly, so the mistress of the château had insisted that they take the Mercedes.

She watched the large wrought-iron gates open automatically and then close. When she could no longer see the taillights of the car, she crossed to a huge walk-in closet.

From a hidden drawer in the rear of a dresser, she extracted a cheap, ankle-length, coarsely woven skirt, a full peasant blouse, a rather ratty cardigan sweater, and a lightweight shawl.

She carried the garments to her dressing room, dropped them on a chair, and let her robe slip to the floor. Beneath the robe was a slender but well-rounded body with small, firm breasts, narrow hips, and long, tapering legs.

She glanced one time in the mirror and then began scrubbing the makeup from her face.

To anyone who knew, a strange transformation was taking place. This woman, who counted on her own beauty above everything, was making herself decidedly plain. The bright blue eyes were made dull. The handsome, pure features were blunted and the spun-gold of her long blond hair was pulled into a severe bun at the back of her neck.

With the addition of the clothes and a pair of well-scuffed, low-heeled shoes, the transformation was almost complete. The final touch was the shawl. A tie at its edges tugged it tightly around her face and under her chin, completely hiding her distinctive hair.

Leaving all the house lights on, she crossed the courtyard and entered the huge garage. Perfectly in a line, their paint and chrome gleaming, were a Rolls-Royce, a Jaguar, and an American Cadillac convertible. She moved past them all to the space usually occupied by the Mercedes.

In its place was a dirty green four-door Fiat of questionable age. There were several dents in the fenders and the upholstery was worn to the springs.

Under the hood, she reattached the two wires she had disconnected that afternoon.

The engine sputtered but idled evenly once it caught. She pulled out of the garage and drove down the long lane. From her pocket she took an electric gate opener and depressed the button on its side. The gate swung open and she flipped on the headlights as she drove through.

On the coast road, she turned east and pushed her speed up to 110 kilometers. An hour later, just inside the city limits of Nice, on the Promenade des Anglais, she stopped at a late-night market.

Randomly she went through the little store until she had enough to fill a good-sized bag.

Back in the car she continued east to the Port Lympia. She parked on the quay and, taking the bag, walked inland from the port on the Rue Arson.

The way she was dressed, and carrying the bag of groceries, she appeared to be a maid or housewife coming home from work after shopping.

It was a neighborhood of tree-lined streets and middle-class apartment buildings. Four blocks from the quay she slowed. Across the street was a four-unit building. In a window of the lower-right unit was a small sticker proclaiming that the occupant had given to the International Red Cross.

The meeting was on.

She checked the street both ways and then crossed. In the dim hallway she found the bell and rang it three short times. In her mind she counted off ten seconds and rang again, this time a sustained ring of ten seconds.

The door opened inward and she darted in, pausing in the hallway only long enough to deposit the bag of groceries on a side table. As she moved into the sitting room, she shook the shawl from her head.

"Good evening."

"Sergei," she said crisply, moving on across the room toward a sideboard.

"There is vodka chilled, if you want it."

"No," she replied.

She poured some vermouth into a tumbler, added an ice cube, and dropped into an overstuffed chair. As she crossed her legs the skirt parted, revealing a thigh clear to her hip.

"Do you have a cigarette?"

He shuffled toward her. "You shouldn't smoke . . . in your profession . . ."

"I know I shouldn't smoke, dammit. Do you have a cigarette?"

"Of course."

He took one from a box on the sideboard, lit it, and passed it to her. She took it and dragged deeply, her eyes following his to her bare flesh. With a nonchalance that suggested that a thigh was of little interest, she adjusted the skirt and, exhaling slowly, spoke.

"If your budget allotment doesn't allow you release, Sergei, I would gladly give you some money."

"What is that supposed to mean?"

"It means you should get a whore, get laid. If you don't have the money, I have."

He turned away, his face crimson. "My sex life is none of your business."

She started to speak, then paused, looking around the room. "You've checked for any devices?"

"Of course," he replied. "I do it twice, sometimes three times a day. You're nervous tonight, tense."

"I'm tired," she said, standing and moving across the room to a floor-to-ceiling bookshelf, "tired of playing the part every waking moment instead of just on the stage."

"It was your choice."

"I know." Her voice was a whisper. She examined the books. They were in French, German, and English, mostly fiction, some good, some bad. "Do you read any of these, Sergei?"

"No. I read only the classics . . ."

"Dostoyevsky, Pushkin, and so on?"

"Yes."

"I thought you would."

Across the room, he lit a small cigar and studied her classic profile. She was beautiful, but probably her most prepossessing feature was her completely relaxed, self-assured manner, that of a woman who looked for and was accustomed to a good deal of attention, mostly from men.

He shook his head to clear it, and spoke. "We have business. What have you learned?"

"I have a name," she replied.

"In East Berlin?"

"Yes. It is Dieter Weist. He is the head barman at the opera."

"Interesting," the man replied, leaning forward in the chair, his mind on this new development rather than the fascinating woman. "You're sure this Weist is somehow connected to the Double X team?"

"Positive. I would imagine he is their cutout. It would be easy for him to pass on the espionage information he receives from Double X. Over three quarters of the weekend audiences for the opera are from East Berlin."

The man nodded. "It's obvious. We should have seen it before. Does he have direct contact with the Double X team?"

"I think so, but there is another courier involved, perhaps a woman."

"You don't have a name?" he asked.

"No."

"No matter. If we cover Weist, he will probably lead us to her. Do you have any more on the team itself?"

"Nothing we haven't already learned. Double X is a man and a woman. They are German, and they have been in place for at least fifteen years. They were turned right from the beginning, and both of them hold responsible positions."

The man sucked on his cigar for a moment in thought. "Were you able to get any more of a timetable out of him as to when they are coming out?"

"No, but I am sure it is soon. They know we are aware of their existence."

He sighed. "It would have helped if you could have gotten a little more out of him."

She shrugged. "He hasn't had direct contact with them for almost three years. Also, he had to be in London this morning for some kind of business conference. He flew out last night.''

''Couldn't you get him to take you with him for a day or two?''

She whirled, her body tense and her eyes flashing. ''No, dammit, I couldn't. What was I supposed to do, tell him I am a Russian spy? 'Please take me with you because I need more information from you? If you're a good boy and tell me what I want to know, you can have my body for two more days?' *Merde!*''

''Calm down, calm down. I know you have done your best. I was only thinking out loud.''

''Well, don't!'' She stomped back to the chair and fell into it.

He stood and gently ran his hand over the golden softness of her hair. ''I am sorry. I know you did your best. We'll get them.''

She only nodded, the anger in her face replaced by weary resignation.

''Would you like that vodka now?''

Again she nodded, patting his hand where it rested on her shoulder.

From a small refrigerator he took a bottle of vodka and two small, chilled glasses. Carefully, he filled the glasses to the rim and handed her one of them.

''To your talent,'' he said, raising his glass.

''Are you referring, Sergei, to my voice or my crotch?''

A pained expression flooded his eyes and spread across his face. The moment she saw it she was sorry for her words.

''To Mother Russia, Sergei.''

They both drank and he refilled the glasses. He lit another cigarette and returned to his chair. For several moments they smoked and sipped the vodka in silence. When she spoke again, her voice was soft, almost a whisper, and she shifted from French to her native Russian.

"Sergei . . ."

*"Da?"*

"You have a wife?"

He nodded. "And three children."

"When did you see them last?"

He looked up from his glass, his heavy brows coming together in a vee. "It will be seven years this month."

"A long time."

"Yes," he said, his teeth grabbing his lower lip, "a very long time."

"It has been twelve years for me." He started to reply, and she held up her hand. "I know. Don't say it. It was my choice. I wanted something and I got it. I have no regrets. It is harder for you than for me, Sergei. I have no husband or children to miss, and God knows I don't miss Mother Russia."

A faint smile curled his lips. "You have a God now, do you?"

This brought a low, husky laugh from her throat. "Oh, no. It is only an expression."

Suddenly she set aside her glass and stood. She moved to stand before him. Slowly she opened her blouse and let it slide from her shoulders. She wore nothing beneath it, and the nipples on her small, firm breasts were erect. She kicked off her shoes and unfastened the buttons on her skirt. With a flip of her hip it fell to puddle around her feet.

He blinked but didn't take his eyes from the dark mound between her thighs.

"Why do you do this?"

"Because, Sergei, I suddenly want to speak Russian again while I am making love."

# TWO

Her street name was Cherry. She was thin and scruffy, with soot-black eyes and clothes that announced her as the hooker she was. Her nails were bitten to the quick and every movement was a twitch. Her arms told the story of her drug addiction.

In the files of the West German police, she was called Katryn. She was eighteen years old.

Nick Carter followed her into the little one-room, barely furnished apartment and closed the door behind him. Out of habit he moved to the window and checked the rain-wet street below.

He had been in West Berlin for six hours and he was pretty sure he had been tagged right from the airport. So far he hadn't detected a tail.

"What do you like?" the girl said, and then laughed hollowly. "For forty marks you get whatever you want."

Carter turned.

She had been wearing a short skirt, summer lace-up boots, and a tight sweater.

Now she was naked, and in the dim light from the overhead bulb he could see that she had been beaten up, recently. Not badly, a few bruises around her body, a cigarette burn on her backside.

"Who did that, your pimp?"

"I don't have a pimp."

"Then who did it?" Carter asked.

She shrugged. "A drunk. He couldn't get it up, so he blames me. Look, you want it or not?"

"Not particularly," he growled, sliding into a wooden straight-backed chair by the bed.

"What? You bastard . . .''

"Settle down." He tossed a fifty-mark bill on the bed. "And put your clothes back on."

She did, just as fast as she had taken them off. She eyed him suspiciously. "You some kind of pervert?"

"Yeah. I want to see Este."

The vacant eyes found fear and the thin body shivered visibly. "Este? I know no Este."

"Bullshit. You lived with him for six months."

"He kicked me out."

"I know that," Carter said, lighting a cigarette. "But you still know how to get in touch with him."

"I might." Her eyes narrowed and she tried to be slinky as she moved around the bed. It didn't work. She tripped grabbing the fifty and shoving it down the front of her sweater.

Carter smiled. He held up a hundred, tore it in half, and shoved half of the bill after the fifty.

"Tell him that Nick the American wants to meet him on business." He stood and moved to the door. "I'll be back tomorrow night around eight. You have it set up."

"What if I can't?"

Carter paused at the door. "Then you don't get the other

half of the hundred, and you get hassled every night for the next month by the police.''

He heard her curse him all the way to the street.

It was raining again when he hit the street, a light, misty drizzle that wasn't cold and didn't soak through. It just gave atmosphere to an already atmospheric Berlin.

A siren wailed directly behind him. It grew louder and an ambulance streaked by, closely followed by a taxi. Carter hailed the cab.

''Haselhorst,'' he said, ''anywhere.''

Twenty minutes later he alighted and walked in circles to further shake off anyone behind him. Then he darted into the U-Bahn and caught the first train. At the Havel station near Spandau, he got off and came back up to the street. Sure now that he wasn't being followed, he grabbed another cab.

''Branitzer Platz.''

An hour and a half after leaving the teenage hooker, Carter stood in the center of the big traffic circle and paid off the driver. When the cab was out of sight with a new fare, he walked down Eichen Allee to number 28.

It was a stumpy, wide but not high, multiple dwelling. There was no downstairs door. Perhaps once upon a time there had been one, but now there was just an open archway to a narrow lobby at the end of which was a narrow staircase. Carter climbed it to the second floor, rang the doorbell of 2C, and waited.

And waited.

He rang again, and finally the shield of the peephole moved and was replaced by an eye.

''Hello, Martin,'' Carter muttered just loud enough to seep through the door.

The peephole closed, the door opened, and Carter was in the seedy living room of a seedy little man in bare feet and a threadbare bathrobe. Martin Bonner was pencil-thin and pygmy-tiny, but he had a ferocious aspect because of a massive outcropping of wild, iron-gray hair that surrounded his head like an exploded halo. It made him look like an angry mop with the wrong end up.

Bonner was the best free-lance forger in Berlin. He worked almost exclusively for the BfV, and consequently for the American CIA. He was paid well and he kept his mouth shut.

"You are looking old, Nick."

"Strain," Carter replied. "I'll take a drink, if you've got a clean glass."

Bonner chuckled. It sounded like a duck in heat. "I can afford better, of course, but the image of the down-and-out, out-of-work printer is good for business."

He scrounged up a bottle of schnapps and washed two glasses. They sat on an ancient sofa that squeaked with every weight shift. Bonner poured, they toasted, and got down to business.

"You go over Friday night. Will you have all your other arrangements made by then?"

Carter nodded. "No problem."

"And the woman?"

"For a night at the opera, she can use her own papers. She goes back and forth often during the season."

Bonner seemed satisfied. "And you won't need my assistance coming out?"

"No. It will be tricky with three of us. I'm going to use Este."

The other man wrinkled his nose. "Is that wise? The man will sell his grandmother's eyeballs for a price."

"I've used him before," Carter said. "He knows better

than to cross me. What have you got?''

"Passport." Bonner dropped a green, red-bordered vinyl folder in front of Carter. "This is the one you'll use once you get loose over there. Your name is Willi Lehman. You're a plasterer from Wittenberg. Here is your travel permit for a five-day holiday in East Berlin. Here's your ticket stub for the train ride from Wittenberg to Berlin." More documents were added to the growing pile. "Here are your party registration papers and your driver's license. As you can see, you wear glasses."

"I'll get some," Carter said.

"You'll stay in Prisen Allee, number One-forty-one. It's a boardinghouse just off Strassburger. The woman who runs it is named Becker, Winola Becker."

"One of yours?"

"One of mine," Bonner said, nodding. "She knows you're coming, but not the reason."

"Winola," Carter repeated. "Isn't that Old German for 'gracious friend'?"

"That's right."

"Let's hope she is."

"She will be. If you need a car, she can take care of it. Anything else . . . money?"

"No, the woman is taking care of that."

Bonner stuck out his hand. "Then, good luck, Nick."

"Thanks, Martin."

Back on the street, Carter went through the process of losing a tail again even though he was sure it wasn't necessary.

It was nearly midnight when he paid off the last of four cabs and walked the final two blocks to her building. It was on a steep hillside overlooking part of the Tegel Forest and the Tegeler See beyond.

She had obviously moved up in the world since the last

time Carter had seen her. He judged the view from the upper floors must be quite a production. And quite expensive.

He entered the sprawling building by a side door. Everything but good taste had gone into the construction of the place. The halls were cool, gray, and dim, and the doors of the apartments were set flush against the walls. None of them had doorknobs, just tiny keyholes, almost hidden. The carpets were deep and they seemed to match the walls exactly. It was something like walking through an endless gray tube.

The apartment he wanted was on the top floor, and after a brief encounter with an elevator with the same decor as the halls, he found it. The door, like all the others, fitted flush with the corridor wall, and not a sign of a knob or a bell button.

The Killmaster knocked.

The door was opened by a woman only an inch or so shorter than Carter, with a bushel of flaming red hair piled high on her head. She had almond eyes, almost Oriental, and they were the color of the sea, deep green with tiny flecks of foam.

She wore a long white dressing gown like a second skin, and from under it vibrations were flowing that would melt steel.

He name was Erica von Falkener. She was thirty-three years old, and she was a modern version of the courtesans of old.

"Just in time to be too late to take me out to dinner." The tone had a bite to it, but the smile was wide.

Carter matched it, kicking the door closed and tugging her to him. "There are all kinds of nourishment."

"Lecher."

"So true."

Her eyes looked even greener in the more subdued light

of the apartment. He lowered his lips to hers. Their lips met, broke away, and met again. He was leaning into her and her body responded. She pressed her full breasts against him and then her hips, moving them tantalizingly.

"Would you like a drink first?" she asked, coming up for air.

"That would probably be more civilized," Carter said with a grin, letting her remove his wet raincoat.

The living room was about the size of a small rail terminal. It was neatly furnished, mostly modern, but with a touch of the exotic here and there.

He moved over to a polished mahogany bar. Behind it he found a full sterling silver ice bucket, a pair of Waterford tumblers, and a freshly uncorked bottle of Chivas Regal.

"Mmm, business must be good," he quipped as he poured three fingers in each glass over a single cube.

"You're crude."

"Am I?" he chuckled, handing her one of the glasses as she slid onto a stool.

"Yes, and I love it."

He had met her aboard the *Queen Elizabeth II,* one night out of New York. They had eyed one another all through dinner. There had been unabashed interest, even lust, in her eyes, and Carter hadn't failed to notice it.

Later, at the bow rail, he had caught the scent of expensive perfume mingled in the salt air and found her at his elbow.

"I love the sea," she said.

A phosphorescent wave gleamed in the sea, reflecting the full moon. A light breeze whipped the filmy material of her dress, plastering it against her body.

He lit a cigarette and she took it from his lips. He lit another.

"Erica von Falkener."

"Nick Carter," he replied.

"American?"

"Yes," he said, and switched to German. "You're a Berliner."

She laughed. "Does it show?"

"Along with everything else, yes."

She had turned to face him, those green eyes penetrating and mischievous. "Are you rich?"

"No, but I get by."

"No matter. I'm on holiday."

A half hour later they were in his stateroom, in bed. He found that she would do anything in bed, and she did it extremely well.

They spent every night of the crossing together, and in that time Carter learned that she was quite wealthy, and had made her wealth from men, some married, some divorced, some widowed. They all had one thing in common, money, and the willingness to part with it in the form of presents.

"I never take cash, only what can be turned into cash."

She was quite open and honest about it, and in the course of their time together they became fast friends as well as lovers.

She never asked Carter what he did, but after aiding him a time or two she had a pretty good idea.

Now she sipped the whiskey, licked a drop sensuously from her lip, and let her negligee fall open. She wore nothing but a strapless bra and panties beneath it.

Carter took in the view and plastered a serious look on his face. "Did my bag arrive?"

She nodded. "In the bedroom. A package came also. It's there, under the bar."

It was a plain envelope with only her name and address on it. Carter broke the seal and spilled a passport and an eight-by-ten photo onto the bar.

"That's my date?" she asked, studying the photo.

"That's your date coming back," Carter replied, opening the passport. "Kurt Heiber, born October 1945, Frankfurt; occupation, dentist."

She wrinkled her nose. "God, my social position."

"For one night," he said laughing, "your reputation can stand it."

She fingered the photo. "Can you actually look like him?"

"Just like him," Carter replied, "That's why he was chosen. His height, weight, and build match mine, and his facial structure is similar."

"Who is he, really?"

Carter leveled his stare. "Do you really want to know?"

She averted her eyes. "No. Let's go to bed."

"Excellent suggestion."

In the even softer light of the bedroom, she turned into an erotic statue. Her breasts were full and thrusting, the curve of her belly warm and inviting, and her legs long and silken.

She peeled Carter's clothes off and then, smiling like Circe, tugged him to the bed. She had a passionate, full-lipped, sensuous mouth, above which was a slender, high-boned, haughty nose.

She was a lady of many contradictions.

They fell to the bed together, and immediately she abandoned herself. Her tongue searched his mouth and her lithe body pressed against his.

His hands moved lightly along her legs, exploring, caressing, awakening nerves and filling her with pleasure. She moaned and opened and closed her hands and thighs. She writhed and murmured nonsense and clasped her fingers in his hair.

Then he was on top of her, flesh against flesh, touching wherever they could.

"You're ready," he whispered.

"I know. Oh God, I know," she gasped.

His lips found her nipples, teasing them gently. Then he swept downward, delicately nibbling and licking. He traced her inner thighs and moved upward.

She cried out and her legs scissored open. "There . . . oh, yes, there!"

Again and again, with no more than the caress of his lips and tongue, he brought her to the peak of arousal and backed away again, making her wait.

And then she could wait no longer. She tugged him upward, reached between them, and guided him inside her.

He moaned as she started rocking under him. He pushed even deeper, eager but determined to hold his pleasure until the last possible moment.

She groaned. Tears streamed down her face, but pleasure pushed those tears back, and soon she gave way to rippling shudders and tiny yelps of pleasure. They rocked together, her hips refusing to allow him to pull away for even the briefest second.

Their movements synchronized, and their breathing matched. They moved as lovers lost in ecstasy, beyond all earthly concerns. They were one as they burst into sensual exultation.

Carter moaned in pleasure as she grasped him in hard little jerks. He kissed her lips, her forehead, her closed eyelids, and her cheeks. She still held him inside her and refused to let him leave. Her body quivered for minutes after their last explosion was over.

# THREE

Carter left the U-Bahn at Potsdamer Platz and walked parallel to the Wall for nearly a mile before turning back, inward, toward West Berlin.

He hit her general cruising area and found her in the fifth doorway he checked.

She looked awful even in the dim light. The lashes were drawn back from her eyeballs as though by some mechanical device, and the pupils were so contracted that the entire eyeball seemed to consist only of smoky iris. A cigarette dangled from the corner of her chapped lips, and even though she wore a trench coat she looked cold.

She spoke in a flat monotone. "Where's the other half of the hundred?"

"Where's Este?"

"The hundred first."

Carter took the torn half of the bill and held it between two fingers in front of her eyes. When she reached for it he grabbed her wrist.

"Hurts!" she howled.

"Este."

"Down there." She inclined her head to the right. "About

19

four blocks. A place called the Dead Horse.''

Carter pushed the torn bill into her hand and the fingers closed over it like a claw.

He moved away without haste, comparing in his mind this poor shell of a girl with Erica von Falkener. They both sold the same product. It was just the packaging and marketing that was so different.

The lovemaking the night before had drained him, but the urgency, compounded by stress, had taken him and the redhead past the threshold of control. Three times during the night Carter had surfaced from fitful sleep, aware that Erica had awakened at the same precise moment. Their move toward each other was simultaneous, the coupling harsh and animal.

He wondered if she was that way with all her men, and hoped that she wasn't.

At the end of four blocks, he paused. Three streets converged, separated by two churches. To his left, down a small alleyway, a pair of cafés faced each other. He spotted the faded sign, Der Tot Pferd, and headed that way.

As he walked, he thought of Este and wondered how the man had survived for so long. For years he had done a thriving black market business by smuggling things into the East. And he didn't stop at East Berlin or the border satellites. It was rumored that Este had contacts to ship jeans and other Western luxuries all the way to Moscow and sell them.

But that wasn't all Este did. He was also a major importer of dope from Turkey and Morocco. And also had a sideline of murder for hire.

All in all, he was a louse. But in Carter's line of work he often had to deal with vermin. And there was no smarter rat than Este when it came to getting people out of the East.

Also, Este owed Carter a favor, many favors. Years before, it had come down to a one-on-one between the two men. Carter had let him live, and the reason was need. He had made it plain that night on a rain-slick Berlin street, much like the one he walked now . . . .

"You're going to live, Este, not because you deserve to, but because I need a slave with your talents. So any time, for the rest of your life, when I call, you come running. You don't come, I come after you."

Twice Carter had made the call, and his slave had come running. He was sure tonight would be no different.

The Dead Horse was like a hundred others in Berlin: small, dimly lit, noisy, and crowded. Canned rock music blared and, on an L-shaped stage in the rear, a bleached blonde with enormous, naked bosoms wriggled lethargically.

It looked as though there was not a single empty table. Twenty marks to a waitress in black tights and a tired red bra took care of that.

She led the way to a table where a teen-age couple sat mooning at each other over a pitcher of beer. She spoke swiftly to them and they immediately left.

Carter ordered, and the tired red bra came back with brandy and coffee.

"All?"

Carter nodded, paid, and added yet another tip. He slowly sipped the brandy and surveyed the room. Finally his gaze came to rest on a table just beyond the dancing woman with the huge, swaying appendages.

There were five men around the table, all hard-eyed, some with prison pallor.

Este was easy to spot. He looked the least Germanic of anyone in the room. He was small and dark, with gaunt, tense features. He was wearing expensive but inconspicuous clothes, and Carter caught the glitter of a big diamond as one hand moved in a gesture.

Carter knew that he had already been spotted; no one would come in or out the door without Este knowing about

it. He sat back and waited for the man to make the first
move. Eventually the little man rose and started drifting
from table to table, doing business.

It was only a matter of time before he reached the Killmaster's table and slipped into a chair. He was scarcely seated
before tired red bra appeared with a cup of coffee. Este
pushed a spoon around in the thick black liquid and stared
at Carter from dead eyes.

"Long time no see. I was thinking you might be dead,
Carter."

"Thinking? Or hoping, Este."

"Both. What the fuck do you want now?"

"Nothing you can't handle."

"I can handle anything."

Carter smiled as he leaned forward. Underneath the table,
his hand found Este's crotch, grabbed, and squeezed.

"Except me, you little son of a bitch."

"Jesus . . ."

"Act tough with your shit friends over there, but drop it
with me, scum."

"Christ, let go of my balls!" he croaked.

Carter released him and lit a cigarette. "I'm going over,
soon. That's arranged. What I need from you is a way back."

"Shit, you don't need that. You know the tunnels."

"No good," Carter said. "Too much risk. I'm bringing
a couple of customers with me, old people. They won't be
able to run if there's a problem. What else have you got?"

Este glanced around the room, grimaced, and began to
talk.

Carter listened. German is a heavy language. One's
tongue had to lumber over verbs and adjectives like a fully
loaded truck over a rough road. The way Este spoke it,
particularly in anger, the language became a swift series of
explosions.

When he finally wound down, Carter shook his head.

"Still no good, Este. Every one of them either has a hole in it or would take too long to set up. Try again."

"Christ, that's it! How many damn ways do you think there are of getting out of East Berlin?"

"More than you've told me."

It took another five minutes of bickering and a hard pat on the knee under the table, but Este finally came through.

"I was going to use it myself, but . . . . Well, there's a plane . . ."

Now Carter was interested. "Go on, little man."

"It's an old Piper Cherokee. They use it to ferry mail to the smaller towns where the jets don't land. It's mostly party stuff, goes out a couple of times a week."

"Yeah . . . ?"

"I have a friend. He has a woman over here. I help him get over to see his woman, he takes back some goodies for me when he goes. For a price he might leave the keys in the plane and a gate open some night."

Carter sank back in the chair, relieved, but he didn't show it. "Can you get in touch with your friend?"

"I'll make a phone call."

He was back in five minutes.

"Let's go."


They moved down a dimly lit hallway that smelled like stale beer and cabbage. At the top of a balustraded stairway they moved down a narrower, darker hall.

"This is it," Este said, and took out a key.

The door opened and they walked into the smell of spilled liquor mingled with perfume and stale body odor. They paused on the threshold to let their eyes adjust, and then went inside.

The apartment was dreary, sparsely furnished with cheap rattan, sisal floor mats, and an old-fashioned iron bedstead by the window with a view of the alley and the next building.

The venetian blinds were drawn and the window was shut. Several bottles glinted in the shadows on the windowsill. They were all empty. Scattered about the room were piles of women's clothing, mostly dirty.

If the woman hadn't moved, Carter would have never seen her. She was curled up in the corner of a sofa with a bottle in her lap. Most of her big, flabby body was bulging out of a torn slip under which she wore nothing. A third of her hair was dirty blond. The rest of it, from the roots out about six inches, was jet black.

"Where is he?"

She looked up with predatory eyes and leaned her head toward a partially opened door. "On the pot."

"Get him."

"You get him," she rasped.

Este struck like a cobra: the flat of his palm across her cheek cracked like a rifle. The bottle fell from her lap as she leaped from the sofa and jiggled through the door.

Seconds later, she returned. Behind her appeared a little man with an acne-scarred face that would always need a shave, eyes that bulged behind thick glasses, and a cigarette in the corner of thick lips.

"You," Este barked to the woman, "out!"

"Where?" she whined. "There's only the toilet . . ."

Este picked up the bottle from the floor and shoved it into her hands. "And close the door."

Again she jiggled out and the door slammed.

Este turned to Acne Face. "This is the man."

"You can fly a Cherokee?"

Carter nodded. "What days of the week do they make their runs?"

"They do the mail on Wednesdays and Fridays. That's the only time it's used unless somebody important has to be flown where the jets don't land."

"Where is it parked?" Carter asked.

Here Acne Face got cagey. "What are you willing to pay?"

Carter almost replied, then thought better of it. "I'll work that out with Este."

"Wait a minute . . ."

Este laid a hand on the man's shoulder. "He'll work it out with me."

He obviously didn't like it but he started talking. "Do you know Schonfeld Airport?"

"Very well," Carter said.

"By the old number two runway, there is a small hangar. Near it, at the end of Bidan Allee, is a large steel gate with a door in it."

"Yes."

"I know where the emergency key to that gate is kept."

"Where will the plane be?"

"That depends on what night you'll be needing it."

Carter did some quick mental calculations. This was Thursday. He would be going over the next evening, Friday. It would take two days at least to make the contacts, even though Double X knew he was coming to take them out.

The last word out from the now-frightened couple had been "Rush."

"Monday night," Carter said.

"So soon?"

"Yes. Can you do it?"

"On Mondays, it will be parked just inside the hangar. It is always serviced just after every flight, so you von't have a problem there."

"What problems will I have?" Carter growled.

"Vopos, guards, two of them. One stays in the hangar office, the other patrols the perimeter of the fence line from there to the main runway."

"I can handle them," Carter said. "Now, tell me about clearance and any traffic I might run into."

In the next half hour, Carter got a complete rundown on everything he might expect to encounter before and after stealing the plane.

At last he stood. "I'll leave you and Este to work out the finances."

Carter left. He stood at the foot of the stairway, smoking, until Este joined him.

"How much?"

"Twenty thousand."

"Fifteen."

"He won't—"

"Bullshit," Carter interrupted. "Fifteen. As it is, you're only giving him five."

"Bastard."

"But an honest one, Este. You'll have your money in the morning. And maybe you had better go back up there and have another small heart-to-heart with him."

"What for?"

Carter raised his right arm and tensed the forearm muscle. A razor-sharp, six-inch stiletto slid into his palm from a chamois sheath under his sleeve. He placed the point just inside Este's right nostril and teased the skin a little until a drop of blood ran down to his lip.

"Because, if that plane isn't there, with the keys and gassed, it's you I'll come back to see, Este. And I'll put this right up through your nose and into your brain."

Carter left him like that, shaking and cursing, and walked into the street to hail a cab.

# FOUR

The extra-watt bulbs Carter had put in sockets alongside the bathroom mirror created an eye-burning glare, but they illuminated every line and pore in his face.

Above the sink he had carefully set out all the materials from the makeup kit. Now, one by one, he started using them.

Meticulously, he worked the putty into his nose until it was much fuller and the bridge wider. Under his upper lip went adhesive gums that made his lip flare out and elongated his smile. A tint that would wear off in a few hours was applied to his teeth until they were stained slightly brown.

Using a single-edged razor blade, he barely broke the skin to make a cut from the corner of his right lip to his chin. Then he waited until the blood had nearly clotted before rubbing a mixture of styptic, clown white, and pancake into the thin wound. When he was finished, only a close medical inspection could prove that it wasn't an old scar.

By the time he finished with his hair, it was flecked with

27

gray, the eyebrows were lighter, and they seemed to grow together over his nose.

The last touch was a pair of contact lenses that turned his dark brown eyes to an opaque blue.

He held up the eight-by-ten photo beside the mirror and compared it to his reflection.

After a little accent with a flesh-colored makeup pencil to accentuate the tiny lines around the mouth and eyes, he was satisfied.

There wasn't a Vopo around Checkpoint Charlie that could tell him from the photograph.

He donned the white-on-white tux shirt and carefully tied the black bow tie. With the suspenders pulled up, and establishing a slight limp in his right leg, he walked into the bedroom.

She was sitting at her vanity putting the last few touches to her hair. She was stunning in an off-the-shoulder black dress that clung to every inch of her full figure. The only jewelry were pearls at her throat and ears.

"Well, darling, are we about ready?" There was a guttural lisp to his voice.

She turned, smiling, and then gasped, both hands going to her throat. "My God, is that really you?"

"It is, Erica dear, and you must act as though you're quite used to this face. Shall we go to the opera?"

For a foreigner to stay overnight in East Berlin—or in any part of East Germany—it takes weeks, sometimes months, of preparation. Permits must be obtained through the ploddingly slow bureaucracy of the German Democratic Republic. Hotel reservations must be made and often approved in advance. The normal everyday tourist who just wants to pop through Checkpoint Charlie for the day and walk the wide Unter den Linden to view the stately buildings, must be back in the West by six that evening. Or, with an extended permit, by midnight.

Those attending the famed, two-hundred-year-old Deutsche Staatsoper have yet another permit that allows them two hours from the final curtain to scurry back through the wall.

These permits were issued at the first checkpoint when Carter presented their tickets.

At the second, final checkpoint, a very masculine-looking woman checked their passport photos against their faces and went over their permits with an eagle eye.

She seemed to take forever. At last she beamed at Erica, sneered at Carter, and passed them through.

A long line of taxis waited beyond the gate to take the operagoers to the theater. Somewhere in East Berlin, a pregnant woman whose water had broken an hour before might be frantically trying to get a cab, but she would be out of luck on opera night. Every cab in East Berlin would be at Checkpoint Charlie.

Operagoers from the West tipped.

They sat back in the cab and Erica slid her arm through his. The light scent of her perfume came to him.

"Hey."

"What?"

"We have a small private box," she whispered.

"So?"

"Want to fool around if it gets boring?"

The darkness hid her eyes from him, but Carter knew they were laughing. "You're incorrigible."

"I know. But since . . ."

Quickly he put a finger to her lips. "The upholstery has ears. By the way, what is the opera?"

*"Boris Godunov."*

"Great," he murmured with less than total enthusiasm.

• • •

It could have been San Francisco, New York, or London. The tuxedos were of the finest cut and the dresses were ultrachic. The jewelry flashed and the people were beautiful.

As usual, the production was spectacular and the talent the best in the world.

But no matter how lavish, *Boris Godunov* was boring. Carter suffered through the first two acts and, at the second interval, squeezed Erica's leg and brushed his lips across her cheek. She did the same, and he was gone.

There were four rest rooms on each tier. The least-used men's room was the one behind the Grand Gallery bar. Carter had a whiskey at the bar and smoked until the first warning chime. He waited for a few more seconds and moved around the bar, weaved his way through the massive pillars, and darted into the rest room.

There was a fat German at one of the sinks and a tall, lord-of-the-manner-type Englishman at a urinal. One set of tuxedoed legs could be seen in the second of six stalls.

Carter moved past the first two men and into the last stall. He dropped his pants and sat.

The fat German stomped out, and seconds later the Englishman left.

The third-act warning chime sounded just as the other stall's occupant lumbered to the sinks. It seemed as if he were taking a bath instead of washing his hands, but finally he finished and Carter heard the door slam again.

He wriggled upward until he was sitting on the tank with his feet on the stool.

The overture to the third act began.

Carter waited.

Five minutes passed, then ten. At last the door opened and Carter heard the rattle of a cart on rollers come across the tile floor, followed by the swish of a mop. It passed in front of his stall and then moved into the adjoining one.

And then he heard it, a faint whistle, the first two bars of "Deutchland Uber Alles."

Carter smiled. It was a gamey recognition signal at least.

He pursed his lips and whistled the next two bars.

Immediately, the legs in the blue coveralls moved into the booth. The coveralls dropped to the floor and Carter's legs came down.

He undressed in time to the other man. As each piece of clothing came off, it was passed under the partition. There was a blue workshirt, a pair of dark, baggy trousers, and a worn vest. Over all of these went the blue coveralls.

The scuffed black work boots were just a tad loose, but Carter remedied that quickly with tissue paper. The last article was a blue work cap, which he pulled down to his ears.

He emerged first and grabbed the mop. Seconds later, the other man came out of the stall. He moved past Carter to the sinks and lightly rinsed his hands. Carter plied the mop until he stood just behind the man's right shoulder.

"Locker number three, right off the washroom," the man whispered in German.

"*Ja*," Carter replied.

For the briefest of seconds, Carter looked up. In the mirror their eyes and their twin faces met.

The man looked shocked.

Carter smiled.

And then he was gone.

The Killmaster gave him a full five minutes and then he too moved back into the hall.

Around the corner to his right he could hear the quiet chatter of the barmen in the Grand Gallery and the occasional clink of glasses.

He went left, to the side service stairs that led all the way down into the lower depths of the great opera house. He passed through two empty rehearsal rooms and then under the stage itself.

Stagehands waited tensely for their cues, balancing huge pieces of scenery on the two elevators that would shoot them upward into place at the precise time.

None of them even glanced at the tall man with the bucket and mop.

Then he was deep in the bowels of the theater, in the boiler room and beyond. He found locker number three, and quickly dumped the cap and coveralls. From the locker he took a worn leather jacket, another cap, and a small canvas pack with straps.

Then he darted into the washroom. Using special soap from a tiny capsule, he washed his hair and face. The blue contacts were discarded, as well as the putty in his nose and the false gums.

The last of the brown stain was removed from his teeth with a finger and a little of the soap.

Then he mounted the stairs again, but this time he moved away from the thundering music coming from the stage. He moved into a rehearsal room with mirrors all around and a waist-high barre at two ends. In one corner of this room was a door. It was a sneak exit often used by stars when they wanted to leave the theater quickly and discreetly and not face their public outside the regular stage door.

Beyond it was a fire escape. At the foot of the fire escape two men, obviously electricians from their tool belts, smoked.

"Almost over?" one of them asked.

Carter shrugged. "How should I know? I clean the toilets, I never hear the music."

They both laughed, and the second man said; "I thought you shithouse cleaners were the last ones out."

"Usually," Carter chuckled, "but I've gotten a

stomachache from the stench of all that rich perfume.''

This provoked hearty laughter and Carter was on the Schmann Strasse walking south quickly. At the Rathaus he turned left and practically ran into two stern-eyed Vopos. One of them eyed Carter's pack but said nothing.

When he reached Alexander Platz, he darted into a café and ordered coffee. For the next hour he sipped coffee and brooded like a good, bored East German.

Directly across the street was the large Café Neva, a popular spot for a late-night snack. It was crowded on opera nights.

Carter waited until the long line of taxis had taken the last of the Westerners back to Checkpoint Charlie, and then left the café.

At the north end of the square he went down into the U-Bahn. He let the Eisenbahn train pass and took the next local.

He walked to the rear of the car where he could survey the car behind. Three women jabbered and an old man sat, his nose in a newspaper.

Carter relaxed, took a seat, and fumbled in a pocket of his leather jacket. He produced a pack of awful East German cigarettes and lit one with a satisfied sigh.

Willi Lehman had arrived in East Berlin from Wittenberg for his holiday.


The train slid into the Tierpark station and the door slid open. Carter walked casually out onto the platform. It wasn't crowded and no one gave him so much as a glance as he headed for the exit.

He walked around the zoo and then picked up his pace. Nine blocks later, he turned onto Strassburger and looked for Prisen Allee.

It didn't take long. It was an old street with old brick

houses that had been only partially restored since the devastation of the war. Number 141 looked to be the oldest of the lot.

Ahead was a heavy door with antique wrought-iron hinges and a studding of old-fashioned nailheads. He used the old, heavy knocker and waited. When there was no reply he knocked again and then backed off to check lights. The windows were all dark in the front of the house, but he thought he saw light in the rear alley.

It wouldn't do to stand out here too long at this time of night. He moved around the corner and along the narrow walkway to the rear.

There was a light and the rear door was unlocked.

He stepped through into the wide, cool dimness of the old-fashioned kitchen, his feet soundless on the Belgian bricks of the floor. Metal glimmered, shining nickel on the big, antique stove. He paused again. No sound except the rattle of wind on the shutters.

Footsteps suddenly clattered down the stone stairs deeper in the labyrinth of the house. They reached the bottom of the staircase and turned his way, soles scraping the floor, slipping and driving on again toward the kitchen.

Carter wasn't sure how, but he knew it was Winola Becker the moment she stepped through the kitchen door. He held his hands out from his side and managed a weak smile.

"Frau Becker, I am Willi Lehman."

She was on the verge of grabbing something to hit him with, but relaxed a bit when he spoke. "Lehman?"

"I think number Seven was reserved for me. I knocked at the front door but there was no answer."

Those were the magic words. The tension faded from her round face and she relaxed completely. "I was preparing your room. This way."

Carter followed her through a sitting room, small and

colorless, crowded with heavy furniture. He couldn't help but notice as she stopped to rummage in a chest that the woman was equally colorless. She was probably no more than thirty-five, but she looked ten years older. She was a trifle on the heavy side, and her body had lost much of its shape. Her wispy blond hair was pulled back on top of her head and there was no makeup on her face.

From the chest she took an old Hasselblad camera in a battered case, and motioned for Carter to follow her again.

They went up the stairs and down a dim hall. She opened the door with a key and Carter followed her inside.

The room felt damp and mildewed by the recent heavy rains. It was a simply furnished cubicle with a metal cot, two wooden chairs, and a metal bureau painted to look like wood. There were no rugs on the bare wood floor.

She snapped on a bare overhead bulb and turned to face him. "All right?"

"Fine," he said nodding. "I don't know how to thank you."

She shrugged. "It is my job. I will need your travel permit."

He passed it over and dropped his bag on the bed. "Were you able to make a connection?"

She held up the camera. "It has been waiting to be put to use for some time."

Crouching by a chair, she pulled a small screwdriver from her apron pocket and removed the camera from the case.

Carefully she disassembled it to yield the aluminum frame and cartridge clip of a 9mm Beretta. The center of the telephoto lens was a seven-centimeter barrel that fitted neatly into the frame. The lens itself was actually a baffled silencer.

Her hands moved swiftly, and in less than ten seconds she held up the fully loaded pistol.

"You can reassemble it?"

Carter nodded. "I can."

"Good." She stood, rubbing the faint remnants of gun oil onto her apron. "One of the boarders is named Grot. Be careful how you talk to him at breakfast. He is MVD. I will return your travel papers in the morning as soon as I have reported them."

"This Grot, is he recent?"

"No, he has been here for some time, but he likes to be suspicious of everybody. Are you hungry?"

"No."

"Some liquor . . . beer?"

"No, just some sleep, thank you."

"All right," she said, dropping the key and the gun onto the bed. "Good night."

She shut the door quietly behind her and Carter stretched out. He lit one of the cigarettes from the crumpled pack and smoked slowly, staring at the spider web of cracks in the ceiling.

Tomorrow he would have his tooth filled.

It was a good thing that everyone, even dentists, worked on Saturdays in the German Democratic Republic.

# FIVE

Carter thought he would hit breakfast early the next morning before any of the other boarders.

He was wrong.

When he walked into the small dining room there were already two men and a woman at the table. He took the empty space. The other three looked up, muttered desultory good mornings, and went back to their food.

The MVD man was easy to spot. He sat directly across from Carter and didn't disguise the studied looks he gave the newcomer as he stuffed food into his mouth.

Frau Becker entered with a plate of sausages and eggs, set it before the Killmaster, and scurried back to her kitchen. He dug into the food.

"Butter . . . marmalade, mein Herr?" the MVD man said, passing the dish.

Carter took it and uttered a small diatribe about the quality of urban food as opposed to the country fare he was used to in his native Wittenberg. He was careful to keep his grammar sloppy and his normal Berlin accent out of his speech.

This seemed to satisfy the MVD man. He finished his

coffee, belched, and left the table. The other man and woman quickly followed.

Frau Becker brought Carter coffee. "That was very good," she murmured as she bent near his ear. "Where did you learn German dialects?"

"I didn't," Carter said with a smile. "Berliners know only their own dialect. Anything different and the speaker must be from the country. They don't know what part."

She laughed. "You'll return for supper?"

"It will depend . . . I doubt it."

She nodded knowingly and left. Carter finished his coffee and walked through the foyer and out the front door. He walked to the U-Bahn and took the train to Marx-Engels Platz. From there he walked along the Spree to Vollner Allee and found number 91.

It was a four-story building that, like so many others in East Berlin, still showed signs of the war.

Dr. Walther Mueller had offices on the top floor. Carter climbed the stairs and entered a Spartan reception room with an old desk, a couple of plastic-covered chairs, and some patriotic posters on the walls.

Behind the desk was a hefty woman in starchy whites with mean eyes. *"Ja?"*

"I have an appointment with Dr. Mueller," Carter replied, biting his tongue as he spoke, as if holding back the pain in his jaw. "Willi Lehman."

*"Ja.* Shortly . . . sit."

Carter sat in one of the chairs and reached for his cigarettes.

"Don't smoke."

"Sorry."

In the States, Carter thought, she would make a good Marine drill sergeant.

The wait was nearly an hour before an old woman, her

cheeks swollen like a chipmunk's, came stumbling out and
the drill sergeant jerked a thumb toward the interior office.

Mueller was around sixty, a small man with rounded
shoulders, faded blue eyes, and stark white hair. He had
been a link in the courier chain since Double X had been
in operation. Before that he had handled other agents in the
East.

"What seems to be the trouble, Herr Lehman?"

"I think I need a filling changed, Herr Doktor." Carter
opened his mouth wide and pointed to three separate teeth.

"I see. And how long have they been bothering you?"

"Oh, since about the seventeenth."

Mueller smiled and Carter could see the relief in his eyes.
"Sit, please." He walked to the door. "Grundel?"

"*Ja, Herr Doktor?*"

"I won't be going out to lunch. Could you run down the
street and pick up something?"

"*Ja, Herr Doktor.*"

Carter could hear the outside door closing, and then Mueller was above him, probing in his mouth with a pick.

"It is good to see you. We were afraid you would not
come."

"A lot of connections had to be made on short notice,"
Carter replied. "What's the situation?"

"There has been no further surveillance on Herr Dorst
and his wife in the past week, but they feel that means
nothing. Surveillance has been taken off their immediate
co-workers as well."

"And you, Doktor?"

"Nothing. If the Dorsts have been blown, there has been
no connection to me."

"But they still want out?" Carter asked.

The dentist nodded and sighed. "Yes. After so many
years, I don't blame them. They are both getting on in years,

and the strain is more each day. Now, since they have been taken off two sensitive projects, one right after another, they feel that the state police are narrowing down their list of suspects. It will be only a matter of time."

"They are probably right," Carter agreed.

Peter and Ruperta Dorst had been in their middle twenties at the end of the war. Both of them had been anti-Nazi, which had thrown them into the Communist camp. From their positions at the Berlin Institute of Scientific Research, they had fed intelligence to the Russians.

After the war they became research specialists in East Berlin. They were loyal to their Russian bosses for years, even after the Wall was erected. Then, slowly, their faith fell apart. In the early seventies, hating what they saw was happening to Germany, they turned. Since that time they had funneled information to the West through Dr. Mueller and the last link, Dieter Weist, a barman at the Deutsche Staatsoper.

The railroad for the intelligence was simple. Once every six weeks or two months, Frau or Herr Dorst would visit the dentist. Both of them had a capped, hollow tooth. In the tooth would be microdots. Mueller would remove them from the hollow interior and replace them with empty ones.

A few days later, after a prearranged signal, Dieter Weist would have an appointment. He would undergo the same process. That night, or soon after, the contents of the tooth would be passed to an operagoer from the West.

The chain wasn't foolproof, but it was as secure as possible. Only Mueller knew about the other two links. Weist knew nothing about the Dorsts, not even their code name.

The dentist was speaking again. "You have made all the arrangements?"

"Yes," Carter replied. "We're flying out."

"When?"

"Monday night. Is that too soon?"

Mueller chuckled. "No. They would go tonight if they could. Where do you want them to be?"

"Do they still have the use of a state car and driver?"

"Yes."

"Good," Carter said. "Have them arrange for a car and driver for Monday evening. They are to tell the dispatcher that they are going to an evening of theater at the Maxim Gorki."

"And . . . ?"

"And I will take care of the rest. What is their address?"

"They have a flat in the Ermeler Haus. Do you know it?"

Carter nodded. "In the Markisches?"

"Yes, number Thirty-four."

"When will you see them?"

"Tomorrow afternoon. There will be an outdoor wedding in the Volkspark and a reception at the Palast Hotel. How shall I tell them to recognize you?"

"I will bring flowers, and my code name will be Jedermann."

Mueller repeated it and nodded. In the hall they heard the clip of the receptionist's heels returning.

"What about you, Doktor?" Carter whispered.

"Me?" He chuckled. "I will go on doing what I am doing. Who knows? Maybe your people already have another mouth that will need a hollow tooth."

The woman walked in carrying a white sack. "Your lunch, Herr Doktor."

"Yes, good, thank you. It's a pity I am not too hungry all of a sudden."

With a smile and a thank you, Carter left the office.

He had some lunch and played tourist the rest of the afternoon. In the early evening he checked out the Markisches area and the Ermeler Haus. Around eight he had dinner in a little restaurant on Stalin Allee.

Figuring that if he had been watched he had more than satisfied his tourist image, he found a little shop that had some better whiskey than the usual Soviet brands. For a small bribe, the owner produced a bottle of decent French brandy. Armed with that and what passed for a newspaper in East Berlin, Carter returned to Prisen Allee and his room.

About eleven, there was a light tap on the door. Carter eased from the bed and put his lips close to it. "Yes?"

"It is me, Frau Becker."

Carter cracked the door and she slid through.

"What is it?" he asked.

"I saw Grot coming out of your room," she replied.

"Does he suspect me?"

"I don't think so," she replied. "He just likes to think he's doing his job. But I was worried about the camera."

Carter smiled. "I had it with me."

"Good," she said, her shoulders relaxing. "I think he would be too stupid to figure it out, but one never knows. Do you need anything?"

"No, everything is fine. It's a waiting game now. I'll definitely be leaving the day after tomorrow."

"Good . . . yes, good."

Carter could sense there was something more from the way she shifted her weight from one foot to the other, the way her eyes darted around the room.

"What is it, Frau Becker?"

"My brother . . . in the West . . ."

"Yes?"

"He is ill, very ill. We are very close. I have not seen him for three years. Would there be any chance . . . ?"

Carter felt a sinking in his gut. How could he tell her that her value was here, that they didn't want her on the other side? How could he explain that a hundred Frau Beckers were not worth the trouble it took to take out one Frau Dorst?

"I'm sorry, Frau Becker, it is impossible."

Her eyes began to fill with tears. She turned her face from his so he wouldn't see it.

"Of course, I understand."

Silently, she moved to the door and let herself out.

Carter stretched across the bed and drank brandy directly from the bottle.


Dieter Weist shrugged into his jacket and left the opera house by the stagehands' exit. The darkness was made worse by the presence of a damp and chilling fog.

Weist was tired. They had run him to death that night. There had been some scenery trouble backstage, and the intervals had been double the normal length.

He was also tense. What was going on? Mueller had told him only that someone was coming over. He had set up the locker the previous evening as he had been told, and found it exactly the same when he had cleaned it out tonight.

Had someone come over? And if he had, what for?

Mueller had warned him the last two times to be extra careful. Why? Was the chain compromised? Were they getting close?

It angered him. If he was about to go up against the wall, he wanted to know about it.

As he left the lighted square, taking his usual shortcut to the U-Bahn station, the fog became thicker, the visibility down to about twenty feet. All he could see was an occasional vehicle and, at times, the shadowy outline of passing pedestrians in the muted blur of widely spaced streetlamps.

At the end of the street he could see the dim light of an outside phone booth. He was near the U-Bahn.

Just past the telephone, a man appeared out of the fog.

"Mein Herr, have you a match?"

"*Ja.*"

Weist patted his pockets and found his lighter. He flicked it, held it to the man's face, and felt the muzzle of a pistol in the center of his gut.

"The car, this way. The door is open."

The gun was transferred to his side and the grip on his elbow was like a vise.

"There," the man hissed, his face so close that Weist could smell his dinner on his breath.

Weist was thrown into the rear of the car, the pistol still pressed to his side. Already in the car was a small, wizened man with a mustache that couldn't hide a deformed upper lip.

"What's going on here?" Weist demanded, realizing it was a futile question. Whatever the answer, he knew he could do nothing about it.

"I am Captain Negatov," said the little man with the mustache.

The moment the man gave his name and rank identifying him as a Russian, Weist knew it was over. The next words were only sound in his numbed brain.

"You are under arrest, Herr Weist."

# SIX

Weist sat in a straight-backed chair darting his eyes from one man, Negatov, to the other, the one who had shoved the gun in his belly and piloted him to the car. He was a big, bullet-headed man with heavy-knuckled hands.

Negatov had called him Metzger. It fit. He looked like a butcher.

Police, Weist thought, come in all shades. There were the loudmouths who sought to break you with shouted confusion, a right-hand swing with fury their only alternative. Then there were the subtle ones, dangerous with false decency. They were the "Tell me the truth, son, and I'll do what I can for you" types.

Weist figured that between these two he had the entire spectrum.

Negatov tapped a cigarette on the face of his watch and placed it between his grotesque lips. He lit it and drew the smoke in with an exaggerated sucking noise.

"Your full name?"

"Dieter Albrecht Weist." The routine was stylized to

stupidity. Though they had a file on you an inch thick, they always started with your name.

"Where do you live?" The cigarette burned steadily as Negatov settled his buttocks on the edge of the desk.

"Number Seven Eisen Platz, apartment Four," Weist replied, carefully keeping his hands relaxed on the wooden arms of the chair.

"You know why you're here, of course, Weist."

"I know nothing."

The room was silent, the labored clanking of a typewriter somewhere nearby clear. The KGB captain moved behind his desk to straddle his chair and lean his chin on its back. "Herr Weist, we know you have used your job at the opera to pass information to an agent of the West. We know that information comes through a cutout, and that it has a high scientific classification."

Weist didn't reply.

"Strip him, search him."

The giant attacked him and in minutes Weist was standing in the middle of the room stark naked. Metzger went to work with a studied thoroughness. He searched the band of Weist's collar, the lining of his tie, his pockets. When that came up empty, a knife was employed and the clothes were cut to shreds. Next came the shoes. The heels were pried off, as well as the soles, and they were cut into pieces.

Then a small, weasel-faced man entered the room wearing surgical rubber gloves, and the ultimate hiding place was probed.

They searched everywhere but Weist's mouth.

His body was covered with perspiration when he again took his seat.

Negatov sighed wearily. "We have two men searching your apartment. If we find nothing there, Herr Weist, we will have to intensify this interrogation. It could be a very long night.''

''I have nothing to say.''

The big man drove the heel of his hand into Weist's jaw. It landed flush, snapping his head to one side and almost driving him off the chair. Weist tried to get his shoulders up to protect his jaw. The interference only enraged the big man and he swung with all his might.

Weist reeled to his feet, trying to turn away. The floor slanted with him and he went down. He was on his knees and elbows with his forehead to the floor.

Negatov got into the act. He came around the desk and kicked Weist alongside the head with a force that drove him back to a kneeling position. Then he kicked him again to send him sprawling with his back against the wall.

''Well, Herr Weist?''

''I am loyal to my country,'' Weist mumbled as blood poured from his lips.

The big man siezed him by the hair and dragged him. He lifted him halfway to his feet and drove a knee to his belly, sending Weist reeling toward the desk. He struck it, falling, its edge in the small of his back.

The two men stood, watching, grinning.

Weist got an elbow on the desk and lifted himself to lean against it. The effort brought pain like a knife lancing through his brain. It made him blind and dizzy. As he waited for it to pass he tasted the salty blood in his mouth. His nose was bleeding and his chest was red and gummy from blood.

Negatov was speaking. ''Take him below to one of the interrogation rooms. Have the doctor examine him and prepare the drugs.''

The giant approached him.

Weist stood quite still, watching the blood form on the tip of his nose and drip to the floor.

He was becoming increasingly light-headed.

His first thought was that it was from a loss of blood. But it wasn't. It was the beginning of a seizure. He could feel it, and knew that the excitement and the beating had brought it on.

*Drugs,* Negatov had said.

That brought a smile to Weist's mangled lips.

If they used drugs, he would die before they would learn anything.

Dieter Weist withdrew his head into his shoulders and willed the pain to subside in his body.

He knew that his nose was broken, and he was pretty sure he had several broken ribs. Through the mist before his eyes he could see his naked body and the purplish welts on his legs from the cigarette burns. He could only feel where they had burned his scrotum.

He wondered if they would use electricity next.

"It's really a shame, Weist, that you are a diabetic. If we could use drugs on you, it would be much easier on all of us."

Slowly Dieter Weist raised his head. The image of the small, dark-skinned KGB captain slowly came into focus.

"I know nothing. This is all a mistake."

"You are a fool, Weist."

Captain Igor Negatov pulled his chair closer, the legs grating over the rough floor. His face was so close that Weist could smell the staleness of his breath.

"Who is Double X, Weist? We know it is a man and woman team. What are their identities?"

"I don't know. I have never heard of Double X."

Negatov was silent for a minute, carefully lighting another

cigarette from the glowing tip of the first one. He inhaled and coughed, the deep cough of a heavy smoker.

"You are a courier or a cutout, Weist. Who do you get your information from and who do you pass it on to?"

When Weist didn't reply, the burning tip of the cigarette was applied to his stomach. From somewhere there was a blood-curdling scream. It was several seconds before Weist realized that it was his own voice, screaming in pain.

"How do you get your information and how do you pass it along?"

No reply.

This time the tip of the cigarette was applied to his left nipple. The whole world was pain now, white, hot, burning pain.

"A drop!" he cried out. "I pick it up from a drop!"

"Where?"

"A call box . . . in Stalin Allee."

"You're lying, Weist. We know you passed three days ago. We were watching you for three days prior to that. You never went near a call box in Stalin Allee."

Weist smiled inwardly. He had never gone near Herr Doktor Mueller in that time either. He had gotten his instructions to ready the locker by phone, the first time that the dentist had ever called him. And he had passed the word to the West on his own that all was in readiness for the penetration.

This time the cigarette caressed his right nipple.

He screamed again, but no words escaped his lips.

And then he passed out.

Negatov stood, cursing in disgust.

"Revive him, keep him awake. What time is it?"

"Just past dawn, around six."

"I am going to sleep for two hours. Then we will start again."

• • •

Carter was crawling up out of sleep when he sensed the door opening. He slitted his eyes and tensed his muscles, ready to spring.

It was Frau Becker, and the expression on her face told him something was wrong.

"What is it?" he asked, sitting up in bed.

"I don't know. A phone call just came for you. It was a man."

"He asked for Lehman?"

She nodded. "He called me by name and told me to tell Herr Lehman that his tickets would be ready early. He said you should pick them up at ten this morning. Do you understand?"

"Only too well," Carter replied, sliding quickly from the bed and reaching for his pants.

Something had gone wrong. The message meant that Dr. Mueller wanted a meeting with him. They were not to meet again unless something urgent came up that would interfere with the next evening's escape.

Five minutes later, Carter was on the street.

Carter took the U-Bahn to the Volkspark stop. Above ground, he crossed the parking lot and headed for the swimming pool.

Sunday morning picnickers were already spreading their food out on blankets beneath the trees.

He topped a hill and spotted the bathhouse, a large stone building with a collage of turrets, arches, and towers. From beyond it he could hear the shrieking of children at play in the pool.

He descended stone steps to a white gravel path lined with flowers. Following the path, he walked behind an immense cluster of rhododendron toward the pool. He swung around it and headed toward the tennis courts and picnic benches beyond.

He spotted Mueller's white-haired head. The old man was seated, alone, at one of the circular tables. A picnic basket of food and an open bottle of wine were on the table before him.

As Carter approached, the dentist was just holding an empty wineglass up to the light, with every appearance that he had just drunk appreciatively.

He had given the sign. He had seen no one suspiciously lurking around, so it was all right for Carter to join him.

"Hello," he said with weary warmth. "Would you like some wine?"

Carter shook his head. It suddenly struck him that the man looked ten years older than he had the day before.

"What is it, Herr Doktor?"

"Weist. The KGB has picked him up."

The man's words fell like a lead weight in the quiet air of the tranquil park.

"When?"

"As near as I can determine, sometime last night. He left the opera shortly after midnight and he never arrived at his flat. I imagine that he has been under interrogation since then."

Carter's guts were boiling but he managed to keep his face expressionless. "That means a good nine, maybe ten hours of interrogation. How well will he hold up?"

Mueller weighed his answer. He reached for the wine bottle and refilled his glass. The bottle was over half empty.

"He's tough, very tough. Also, I know for a fact that he is a diabetic. They won't use drugs because they won't want him to die before they get information."

"But we don't know his threshold for pain."

"No. But I'm inclined to think that Dieter will die before he will talk."

Suddenly, the children's shrieks from the swimming pool seemed muted. The smell of the earth around them seemed stronger than the pungent odor of the flowers.

Mueller seemed to be absolutely at ease. He picked up his glass of wine, tasted it, and set it down. He regarded Carter with what appeared to be honest curiosity.

"What do you propose?"

"We'll go tonight," Carter replied.

Mueller nodded. "I thought so. I will pass the word at the wedding." He checked his watch. "And that is only two hours from now."

He stood, straightened his jacket, and dropped an arm on Carter's shoulder.

"Herr Doktor, there will be room on the plane for three passengers."

Mueller chuckled. "No, my friend. There is very little for me here, but less over there. Good luck."

Carter waited until Mueller was completely out of sight before he himself left in search of a flower shop.


Weist lay on the cot barely able to make out the ceiling of his cell through his swollen eyes. He had been interrogated seven times. Each time was worse than the one before.

He wished he was dead.

But he wasn't.

He was alive. He felt as if he were swimming in his own blood. His naked body was a mass of tortured nerves. His face was mangled, his jaw broken, and he was pretty sure that he had lost his right ear.

But he had told them nothing.

Now he lay on the cot in silence and waited for the sound of footsteps striking the concrete floor of the long corridor toward his cell. His mouth was open, gaping, as he raspingly drew breath.

And waited for the eighth interrogation to begin.

There was nothing he could do but wait. Sooner or later, he knew with a sense of sick inevitability, he would hear the footsteps and knew they were coming for him.

Dimly, he wondered why he was allowing these swine to do this to him. He had only to tell them what they wanted to know and they would stop. They would kill him, of course, but the pain would stop.

Negatov had spoken to him like an older brother or a father. "Save yourself, Weist. Why suffer needlessly? Just tell us what we want to know."

A hundred times it had been on his lips: *Mueller*. But he hadn't spoken it aloud.

At first he held out because he considered himself stronger than they. Then it became sheer perversity. Now it was because he just didn't care. He had reached that plateau where the pain had a calming, numbing effect.

He was just waiting, and willing, to die.

That was the real reason why he defied his interrogators and why, half-man that he was now, he crouched forward in abject fear on the cot in his cell and in terror awaited the sound he dreaded most.

The footsteps, hard and heavy and unrelenting, across the floor.

And that was the real reason why, although he crouched in fear, although his body was on fire with pain, although he could stop the torment if he would only speak out, that was why he held his tongue and, except for uncontrollable cries of anguish, was silent before his inquisitors.

The footsteps came and he knew they were coming for him.

He said, "No," at first under his breath, and then louder, louder.

"No!" he shouted.

In one of the other cells a woman began to scream hysterically.

*"No!"*

The footsteps didn't pause or faulter. They reached the door of Weist's cell. A key rattled in the lock. With morbidly fascinated eyes he watched the door swing outward.

"No . . ." he said again, his voice quiet but trembling now.

Negatov stood in the doorway, a leering smile on his face. Grinning evily at his shoulder was the giant, Metzger.

"It is over, Weist."

The mangled man on the cot only grunted.

Negatov came forward. He leaned over Weist until their faces were only inches apart. The man's eyes gleamed with a bright, feral light.

"The doctor examined your jaw, Weist. To repair it so you could talk. He had to remove your teeth. This is what he found."

The face disappeared. In its place Weist saw a thumb and forefinger. Between them was the hollow tooth.

"It is only a matter of time now, Weist, now that we know. The work on the tooth is excellent. I will commend its maker when he is found. Good-bye, Weist."

Dieter Weist felt the sudden jab of the needle in his neck.

Seconds later the pain ebbed, and for just a few seconds before he died, he felt complete calm.

# SEVEN

Peter Dorst was old, but his skin looked older, and his eyes looked oldest of all. They were wise and heavy-lidded and feathered with fine wrinkles at their corners. They were calm eyes, never given to surprise. They had looked their fill on human guile, wickedness, and depravity, and seen it all. It was unlikely that anything could now occur to astonish them.

They were not astonished now as their owner stood in a small grove of trees, puffing on a pipe and listening calmly as his old friend and comrade, Walther Mueller, gave him the instructions.

"And so," Dorst said finally, "after all these years it is over. We leave tonight. We retire."

"They have all the arrangements made, Peter," Mueller said. "A new identity. A small cottage in England. You can spend your days growing roses."

Dorst chuckled. "After all this time, dear friend, what else could I do? Deception is all I know . . . besides growing roses. And you, Walther?"

The dentist shrugged. ''I may still have time for more deception.''

''But Weist . . .''

''I don't think Dieter will break. He's a good man. He knows the game. I think he will die before he gives me away.''

''Let us hope so,'' Dorst said, extending his hand. ''I will go and tell Ruperta that we leave tonight. I know she will be glad.''

Mueller only nodded.

Silently he prayed that Dieter Weist had the strength to die before he talked.


The connection Este had taken Carter to meet in the whore's West Berlin apartment was named Klaus Pahlmann. He lived in an alley off the Invaliden, in an apartment above a garage. The garage was run by Pahlmann's brother, and Carter hoped they would be closed on this Sunday afternoon.

Carter, a box of flowers in his arms, stood across from the garage and surveyed the nearly empty street. All appeared to be well; there were no loiterers, no lurking figures in doorways or watching the street from windows.

The big main door was closed, but there was a small door, which Carter tried. It was unlocked. He opened it and slipped into the dark interior.

All around him was the general smell of autos, grease, oil, and rubber. Through the maze of several cars in various stages of repair, Carter could see an office in the rear with a light.

As he drew near, the Killmaster saw that the office door was open, but there was no sound of talk or movement.

Planting a big smile on his face, he tapped on the frosted glass and stepped into the room. A sturdy, froglike man sat knees-apart-feet-together on a stool. On a table before him was a chessboard that he studied intently, scarcely glancing up when Carter entered.

"*Ja?*"

"I'm looking for Klaus. You must be his brother."

"*Ja.*"

Carter waited. When he got no more of an answer, he spoke again. "I have owed him some money. I have come to pay."

Suddenly the little man's face came alive. "My worthless brother owes me a small fortune. You can pay me."

Carter backpedaled. "I would like to apologize to Klaus for taking so long to pay."

The man mulled this around in his small brain for a moment, stood, and walked to the door. "He is up there, in the loft. He got very drunk last night, as usual, so he's probably sleeping."

"Thank you."

Carter was almost to the wooden stairs when the man's voice stopped him. "How much do you owe him?"

"A hundred marks."

The man nodded, smiled, and went back to his chess game.

The partitioned loft was shabby. Klaus Pahlmann lay sprawled across the dirty bed in his underwear. Carter was almost to the bed when Pahlmann's eyes opened. They tried to focus on Carter, but without his glasses he could only stare until the Killmaster was right over him.

"You! *Mein Gott*, are you mad . . . ?"

Carter clamped a hand over his mouth. "Klaus, Klaus, old friend, how are you? I've come to pay you the money I owe you!" he called loudly. Then he added in a whisper, "Keep your voice down. Do you understand?"

The eyes focused, but none of the color returned to the face as Pahlmann nodded. Carter removed his hand.

"Damn fool, you'll have us all arrested!" Pahlmann hissed.

"Not unless you screw up," Carter repliled. "Things have changed. We have to go tonight."

By now Pahlmann had put his glasses on and was digging out a crumpled cigarette pack. At Carter's words he glanced up sharply. "Impossible! The hangar doors are closed on Sunday—everything is locked up. Any activity and the walking patrols would know something was wrong!"

"Monday is out. We have to go tonight." Carter withdrew a wad of bills from his pocket and dropped them onto the bed. "A bonus, two thousand marks."

Pahlmann's watery eyes devoured the bills and then looked up at Carter. It didn't take him long to weigh the money along with the risk and opt for the former.

"I don't have the duty tonight, but I can make a call and switch with someone."

"Good."

"The problem is that a second plane, a Stutz, is parked in front of the Cherokee. I can't shift them around. Can you fly a Stutz?"

"If it flies," Carter growled, "I can fly it."

Metzger replaced the telephone and scratched seven more names off the sheet in front of him. Across the desk, Captain Negatov mashed out his cigarette and spoke.

"How many more to go?"

"One hundred forty-two," the big man replied. "God, I didn't think there were so many dentists."

"Can we get more men?"

"We have nearly a hundred on it now. The problem is Sunday. We are breaking into those offices where we haven't been able to contact anyone, but in some cases the record and appointment books can't be found."

Negatov nodded. It was a pleasant, warm Sunday. Dentists, even in East Germany, were well paid. Most of them would be spending a day in the country with their families.

"If the dentists can't be found, go after secretaries, receptionists."

"*Ja, Herr Kapitän.*"

Metzger reached again for the telephone to get in touch with the field leader of the search teams.

Negatov had really screwed up this one, he thought. The hollow tooth was too much of a long shot. The cutout didn't necessarily have to be a dentist.

Metzger would make sure that in his own report he made a notation that he had urged further interrogation of Weist before he was terminated.

Grundel Hagan felt physically ill as she was handed from the car and escorted into the building by two men. They had taken her away from her parents' table with no explanation. But then the police never gave explanations.

"We must go to Herr Doktor Mueller's office at once," they had said.

"But why . . . on Sunday?"

"The car is waiting."

At the office door her hands were shaking so hard that she couldn't get the key in the lock. One of the men did it for her.

"Where do you keep your appointment book, Fräulein?"

"There, in that cabinet."

"Get it."

She had the same trouble with the file drawer, but finally it was opened and the thick book was placed before one of the two men.

For the next hour Grundel sat primly on the edge of the chair while the one at the desk—a gawky person with a

painfully thin face and a brown mop of thinning hair—
poured over the appointment book.

The other one, a husky blond with mean eyes, smoked
and leered at her legs.

Neither of them spoke.

At last the gawky one slammed the book closed and stood
with a disgusted sigh. "Nothing," he said to his partner,
and started around the desk. "You may put the book away,
Fräulein."

Grundel Hagan was halfway to the file cabinet when the
husky one spoke for the first time. "That is your only
appointment book, isn't it, Fräulein?"

"Yes . . . except for the logbook."

"Logbook? What logbook?"

"We keep a daily log of every patient treated. When we
have an emergency, the patient is logged but they wouldn't
be in the appointment book."

"Quickly, Fräulein, let us see the logbook."

Afternoon was turning to evening when the gawky one
dived for the telephone and barked his findings into it.

The door opened at the first knock. The woman was
small, with sparkling eyes behind rimless glasses. Her hair
was gray with a liberal coloring of blue rinse giving it a
peculiar sheen in the light. She wore a primly cut, high-
collared black dress with a single strand of pearls around
her throat. She held one arm behind her back.

"*Ja?*"

"Frau Dorst?"

"*Ja?*"

"Flowers, Frau Dorst, from Jedermann."

The words had barely left Carter's lips when Peter Dorst
stepped from behind the door. In his hand was a Makarov

automatic. His wife's hand appeared at her side holding its twin.

"Come in, hurry!"

Carter stepped into the foyer and the door was quickly closed behind him. "Herr Dorst, Frau Dorst, I am happy to meet you both."

"What may we call you?" the old gentleman asked.

"For now, call me Willi."

"I understand."

"Have you ordered the car?"

"Yes, for seven-thirty. They are always prompt."

Carter checked his watch. "Then we shall relax as much as we can for the next half hour."

The old woman lifted the box of flowers from Carter's hands. "I'll just put these in water."

The two men exchanged smiles as she moved into the depths of the apartment.


Dr. Walther Mueller stood at the window of his study peering down at the street through a crack in the drapes. He had been at the window for two hours, with only a five-minute break to relieve himself.

When he saw the two cars pulled sideways at each end of the block, and the black Volga sedan pull to the curb across the street, he sighed. It was almost with relief.

It had been too much to hope that Dieter could hold out against them. They were ruthless, and they had centuries behind them in the fine art of interrogation and torture.

But they would be beaten yet.

Taking his glass of brandy, he went to the front door. When he was sure all three locks were secure, he moved into his bedroom. He kissed the fading picture of his beloved wife gone these twenty years, and drank the brandy.

Then he climbed onto the chair he had set in the center of the room.

With a last glance at the picture, he carefully placed the noose around his neck and tightened the knot.

The two of them, the old man and the old woman, stood coatless before the door. When the knock came, Carter flattened himself against the wall and nodded to the man.

The door opened.

"Herr Dorst?"

"*Ja?*"

"I am your driver. The car is below."

"We are not quite ready. Would you care to step inside for a glass of schnapps while you wait?"

"Thank you, mein Herr."

The couple backed off and a tall, rangy man in a dark suit and hat filled the space.

Some instinct must have warned the man. Just as Carter threw a chop at the softness behind the back of his right ear, he ducked. The blow missed, striking his shoulder, and he tried to retreat.

Carter thrust his leg forward, caught the other's ankle, and the bolting figure spilled headlong across the floor and crashed into a large oak table.

Carter dived.

The man was a driver, not a fighter. When he rolled around to face his attacker, his features were convulsed with obvious terror. His hat had fallen off and his straw-colored hair was disheveled. His eyes were wide dark holes that reflected his fear as he fought against Carter's weight.

His fist caught the side of the Killmaster's head and made his ear ring. Then Carter had his flailing arms pinned to his sides. With a grunted effort Carter hauled the man to his feet and slammed him against the wall.

Panic broke the dam of fear that had built up in the man's mind. He made a queer screaming sound and lunged at Carter, hands like claws that scratched at the Killmaster's face.

Carter ducked and threw a hard right that crunched solidly into the man's face. He struck again, and the man slammed against the wall with a thud. He lost his footing and slid to the floor, his back to the wall.

Carter started to straighten him up again and then paused, satisfied.

The driver was out cold.

Frau Dorst appeared at Carter's side. "Is he dead?"

"No . . . out. Get the sheet you ripped into strips and the adhesive."

As she hurried away, Carter stripped off the man's coat and pulled it on. It was a little tight, but it wouldn't hamper his movements enough to bother him.

Frau Dorst returned with the long strips of sheet and the adhesive. As Carter and the old man tied up the driver, she got their coats and the small bag of valuables and mementos they would take with them.

At the door, the old couple paused, their arms around one another, looking at the apartment and then at each other.

"I think, folks," Carter said, "we really should be going."

"Yes, we really should," Dorst said, and, holding hands, they followed Carter down to the street and the car.

Negatov knew that the chances that he would find Mueller at his home were slim, but it was all he had. Dragging deeply on his hundredth cigarette of the day, he urged the driver to go faster.

Before the Volga sedan was completely stopped he was out of the car and running. He burst through the front doors and up the stairs with Metzger, the prison doctor, and two agents right behind him.

He screamed at the slowness of the elevator and the dimness of the hall when they reached the tenth floor. At the end of the hallway was a heavy wooden door. Negatov trained his flashlight on the door.

"Break it down!"

It took three shoulder smashes from Metzger and one of the agents before the jamb splintered and the door fell inward. Negatov was in the room before the door hit the floor.

He flicked a light switch and got nothing.

The living room and the study beyond were empty. He bolted for the open door of the bedroom, leading with the flash.

The beam fell on the legs of a man. They dangled before him, the feet only inches off the floor.

Negatov raised the light, and it fell on the tightly wound noose of a twisted sheet wrapped around the man's neck. Mueller hung from it, his head bent awkwardly to one side.

Negatov jumped forward and grasped the body, lifting it. "Cut him down!"

One slice from Metzger's knife and the body sagged. The KGB man lowered it to the floor and dropped to his knees beside Mueller. He was still warm, but there was no heartbeat, no pulse.

*He's dead,* Negatov thought angrily, and then screamed it: "The son of a bitch is dead!"

"Perhaps not," the prison doctor said, shoving Negatov out of the way.

The doctor flipped Mueller over into position on his face and was leaning forward to press air from his lungs, leaning back lifting his arms, and then pressing forward and down again. Mueller had stopped breathing, but so do men who drown, and often they can be revived. He kept working on him, losing track of time. They knew that Mueller could have been unconscious only briefly; the breath couldn't have been kept from his lungs and body and brain for very long. But still he lay motionless.

The doctor kept on . . . and suddenly got a slight response from Mueller, a faint gasp for air. He continued the artificial respiration, and then Mueller was breathing unaided. His hands moved, and then he stirred. In a moment his eyelids fluttered. Soon his eyes opened and he tried to sit erect. The doctor started to help him, and Mueller let out a yell and swung a hard fist at his face.

The doctor ducked aside, the knuckles grazing his cheek, then grabbed Mueller's arms and tried to hold them. Mueller was surprisingly strong for a man just brought back from unconsciousness . . . from death, for that matter. He was shouting and straining against the doctor's arms, trying to slug him.

Then Metzger and the other two agents jumped into the melee, and in no time Mueller was subdued, helpless on the floor.

Captain Negatov took the prison doctor aside. "How long, after the drugs, can we get him to talking?"

The doctor shrugged. "A matter of minutes."

"Make it seconds, Herr Doktor."

# EIGHT

The car was a Volga M-124, small but sleek and fast. It was all Carter could do to force himself and keep the machine at a steady speed.

As they moved through the warm night in a roundabout way to Schonfeld Airport, the Dorsts, from the back seat, kept up a running commentary. The subject was their betrayal. They were both positive that they had not been blown from any brilliant investigative work on the part of the KGB or the East German security police.

"Quite the contrary," Herr Dorst muttered. "We were blown from the West. Too few people knew of us, knew our identities."

"What about Weist and Mueller?" Carter asked, maneuvering the car around a line of trucks.

"They, too," Frau Dorst replied. "We were a team, the four of us. Not over a half-dozen people in your government knew of our existence, let alone any of our names."

Carter listened and digested. It wouldn't be the first time somebody screwed up and blew a couple of good agents. He didn't say as much to the old couple, but he was already filing everything away in his mind that he planned to investigate when they got out of this mess.

Breaking down doors had become Metzger's specialty that night.

When it was done, Negatov again led the way, lunging into the darkened apartment, a gun in one hand, a flash in the other.

They were in the middle of the living room, crouching, listening, when they first heard it, a muffled cry, like that of a wounded bird.

"You two, the kitchen!" Negatov growled. "Metzger, follow me."

They ran the length of the hall and burst into the bedroom. It was empty. Negatov started to turn back, when he heard a low, guttural moan like that of a trapped animal.

"The closet," Metzger rasped, already moving toward the closed door.

It was yanked open. On the floor of the closet was a man trussed up with torn strips of sheet. Half of his mangled face was obscured by a wide strip of adhesive, through which he was trying to speak.

Negatov ripped the adhesive off and roared at the man on the floor. "I am Captain Igor Negatov, central unit, KGB. Who are you?"

"Zeisman, Ruger Zeisman. I work in the motor pool. I was sent to pick up Herr Dorst and his wife and take them to the theater."

"They did this?"

"No, there was a man, a big man, behind the door when I walked in . . ."

Negatov listened, urging the man to tell more and tell it faster, with quick, precise questions. When the driver finished, Negatov turned to Metzger. "They are making a run for it. The man who did this must be the American they sent over to bring the traitors out. Zeisman . . . ?"

"Yes . . . yes, sir?"

"Your car . . . and the number?"

"A black Volga M-124. Four doors. The number is AR41-43."

"Metzger, alert the Wall. I want everyone out and every light on. Also, I want every motor and walking unit in the city alerted to that car."

*"Ja, Herr Kapitän."*

"Also, they might try to get deeper into East Germany and out another way. Block all the roads, *all* of them, leading out of the city."

*"Ja, Herr Kapitän."*

Metzger rushed out to radio the new information. Negatov searched the apartment for a telephone. A man of Dorst's position would surely have one.

He was right. It hung on the kitchen wall, and thankfully it worked.

Quickly he dialed KGB Central on Unter Den Linden, and nervously tapped a countertop with his long nails until a clerk picked up and answered in a bored voice.

"This is Negatov. Put me through to Crofus at once!"

A series of clicks and a husky bass voice came on the line. "Crofus . . ."

"This is Negatov. Have you magnified the tape of the Mueller interrogation?"

"Most of it, Herr Kapitän," came the reply. "You must have used too much of the drug. Much of what he said is rambling, incoherent."

"Then there is nothing new?"

"Not much. One thing, perhaps. Twice he mentions escape in conjunction with flying."

"Flying?" Negatov roared. "The only flights out of

Schonfeld are Aeroflot direct to Moscow. They are not trying to escape to Moscow!"

"I am sorry, mein Herr. I can only tell you what I am able to hear."

Negatov slammed the phone back onto its wall cradle and sprinted toward the front of the apartment. Behind him he heard the agonized wails of the driver, Ziesman, begging to be released.

He paid no attention.

"Metzger!"

The big German was barking orders into a portable unit. *"Ja, Herr Kapitän?"*

"Schonfeld. Put more units around the airport and beef up security inside!"

*"Ja, Herr Kapitän."*

"And have a helicopter ready. I'm going out there."

*"Ja, Herr Kapitän."*

Negatov hurried toward the street, a sinking feeling in his gut.

*Flying?*

What the hell were they going to fly?

Carter parked the Volga in a cul-de-sac off Bidan Allee. Beside them, a small stream meandered toward the Spee. Two hundred yards beyond the stream was the rear of Schonfeld. Nearly two miles in the distance he could see the tower and the lights of the terminal.

The two new, major runways were well lit. They were also far in the distance.

"Follow me!" he said.

The two older people splashed behind him across the stream and through the trees on the other side. On the very edge of the trees Carter called a halt and crouched down.

He spotted the big gate and the smaller door in its center.

The gate was conventional, insufficient in itself to serve as a bar to anyone intent on entering. But it had been laced with barbed wire, and there were heavy wooden beams backing it up.

Extending from the pillars in both directions was a stockade of hardwood posts, each as thick as a man's thigh. The chain link from post to post was ten feet in height and strung in alternate and loose strands along the top.

Making matters worse, all the brush and trees had been cleared from around the fence, leaving an area of sixty or seventy yards perfectly smooth and free of any cover. Only in a particularly heavy darkness could one approach the gate without being seen.

Thankfully, only a few interior lights were burning in the hangar. The cleared area outside the fence was in darkness.

"Herr Dorst . . ."

"*Ja?*"

"Do you see that door in the gate?"

"I see it."

"I have a man inside. Hopefully, that door is unlocked. I'm going in. I want you and your wife to stay here, in the cover of these trees. When you hear the sound of an airplane engine start up, I want you to run for that gate. Can you do that?"

The old man looked at his wife. She smiled. "We can do it."

"Good," Carter said. "Once you get through the gate you'll see me taxiing the plane."

Dorst's brows knitted as he stared at Carter. "Willi, what about guards? Surely there will be someone around . . ."

Carter returned the old man's stare. "There will be, but I will have taken care of them. One more thing. If you hear shots and within a few minutes you *don't* hear the engine of the plane, get out."

"Get out?" Dorst said with a chuckle. "Get out where?"

Carter gave him the name of Winola Becker and her address in Prisen Allee. "She will hide you until they can send someone else."

Carter took a deep breath and sprinted across the open ground. He paused only a second to listen at the door, and then tried it.

It was unlocked.

He darted through, closed it silently behind him, and dropped to the ground.

Fifty yards away, two sodium vapor lights on tall poles illuminated the front of the hangar and the concrete apron leading to the runway. A bare bulb gleamed through a small window on the far side of the hangar. That would be the office.

Carter went over both conversations with the bespectacled and acne-faced little man:

There would be one, perhaps two security guards in the office besides himself. Once every hour or so, one of them would take a turn around the outside of the hangar area.

Also, there were two perimeter guards on the fence using flashlights as they made their rounds. They left the hangar every hour, usually on the hour. One turned to the left and made a casual loop, the other right and followed a mirror-image route.

When they reached the opposite ends of the runway, they retraced their steps.

No matter how hard Carter peered along the fence line, he couldn't see their lights. That meant one of two things. They were either in the hangar office taking their break, or they were at the far ends of the runway.

Either way, Carter was not about to waste time locating them.

He began crawling forward on his belly.

• • •

Corporal Hermann Veggan angled his battered Volkswagen along the quiet street and through the uneven row
of decaying buildings on either side.

It was a sorry car for patrol duty. One headlight blinked
on and off, the other was so dim that it didn't illuminate
the road. And the radio was worse. All it produced was
static. He always patrolled with it off until he had to report
in on the hour.

It was off now.

In the dark, with the full moon lending a milky glow to
everything in sight, it seemed as if this end of the airport
were haunted. That was why Veggan liked his duty. He
could stop any time he wanted for a smoke or a quick nap
during his tour, and no one would be around to catch him.

He turned in to his favorite napping spot, the dead end,
Bidan Allee, and hit the brakes.

There, at the end of the alley in the cul-de-sac, was a
Volga. He knew from the license plate that it was an official
car.

Tonight, with a KGB Volga in the area, was no time for
a nap. Quickly, Veggan reversed and backed out onto the
larger road. As he chugged away, he checked his watch.

He had to report to headquarters in five minutes. He
turned on his radio. As usual, he got only static that hurt
his ears. He shut it off.

As usual, he would have to use the phone booth by the
main terminal when it was his turn to report in.

As he drove over a set of railroad tracks and followed
the curving roadway around the airport, Veggan wondered
if what he often heard was true.

Did everything in the West actually work?

Carter was ten yards from the door when it burst open

and a uniformed Vopo, his machine pistol slung across his chest, came out onto the concrete apron. He paused only long enough to slam the door behind him, and then headed directly to where the Killmaster crouched, just beyond the arch of the sodium vapor lamp.

He was only two feet away when Carter came up out of the shadows. The Killmaster missed the throat with the balled, extended knuckles of his left hand. The blow smashed into the center of the man's face. Carter could feel the cartilage of the nose give way, and saw blood spurt.

There was an angry groan of pain. Before the groan could turn into a shout of warning, Carter used his right. It was a direct hit, right in the windpipe.

The man staggered back and the Killmaster moved in to set up the kill.

The guard must have guessed that this was going to be it. Suddenly he tried to turn and run. He hit a patch of mud on the edge of the concrete and his foot slipped.

As he went down, Carter nailed him with a brutal chopping blow to the back of the neck.

The ferocity of the blow brought Carter to one knee. He stayed like that for several seconds, listening. Satisfied that the sound of the scuffle had alerted no one, he went to the tips of his toes and peered through the thin rail of glass in the big hangar door.

They were both there, the Stutz, with the Cherokee directly behind it, gleaming dully in the dim glow of a night light over a rear workbench.

Crouching again, Carter moved to the doorway. Beyond it the hall was dark, a sliver of light seeping from beneath the door of the office.

He moved on until he was directly beneath the window. Cautiously, he raised his head until his eyes were just over the sill. Inside, a tall, muscular youth was splashing water onto his face over a sink. A holstered revolver sat on a nearby table, and a machine pistol was slung over the back of a high-backed chair.

The Killmaster moved back to the door and into the hall. To his right, through a pair of swinging doors, was the interior of the hangar. He could hear or see no one. To his left was the office door.

He put one hand on the knob and the other on the butt of the Beretta assembled from the pieces of the Hasselblad.

Then he thought better of it.

A shot from an unsilenced gun would bring the two perimeter guards at a dead run.

He would have to take this one as he had taken the first one, with his hands.

Boldly, he opened the door, stepped in, and walked toward the sink. The guard was just reaching for a towel. He muttered a name Carter didn't catch, and just before the Killmaster reached him, dropped the towel from his eyes.

Alarm flashed in his eyes. He threw the towel and, in the same movement, dived for the machine pistol. Carter toppled the chair with a kick and got a solid punch in, just above the man's heart.

The guard staggered, but the blow wasn't enough to drop a man of his size. He bellowed like a wounded bull and charged, punching with both hands.

He was almost there when Carter dropped to the right. Punching at air, the guard went right by. Carter slammed him with a left. It landed dead center in the face. It almost sank in, as into soft jelly. Carter smashed his right, bladelike, down on the guard's neck.

The man toppled to the floor like a felled tree, his eyes glazed, and stayed there.

"Are you going to kill him?"

Carter whirled. Zeisman stood in the doorway. He wore

gray mechanic's overalls, and his mouth gaped. Behind his glasses the eyes seemed to be rolling around in their sockets.

"No," Carter replied, "there shouldn't be any need for it. He'll be out for at least twenty minutes. That should do it. I'll be gone by then. Is the Stutz fueled?"

The other man nodded. "And checked out."

"What about the two perimeter guards?"

Zeisman's eyes went to a big, round clock on the wall. "They left about twenty minutes ago. They should be at the ends of the runway now, making their turn."

"Good enough," Carter growled. "Let's get into the hangar."

Zeisman turned and started down the hall, speaking over his shoulder. "You'll have to give me time to get over to the terminal. If I'm here when you leave, they will wonder why I didn't try to stop you."

"No, they won't."

"Of course they—"

That was as far as he got. Carter chopped him twice behind the ear and he hit the floor.

# NINE

Corporal Hermann Veggan lit a cigarette as he strolled listlessly toward the telephone. He was five minutes late reporting, but on a dead night like this he was sure there would be no repercussions. More than likely, most of the watch at Central sector were asleep or in the canteen.

He unlocked the box, grabbed the spindly phone, and hit the single button.

The voice was there instantly, and tense. "Central, go ahead."

"Corporal Veggan, sector ten, two-hour check."

"Veggan, you ass, where have you been!"

"Where have I been? I've been patrolling my sector—"

"Why didn't you respond when I called you on the radio?"

"My radio gets nothing but static. If you'll check, you'll find that I have put in eleven requests for a new one so far this year."

"All right, all right. Listen good, we may have a Code Seventy."

*Good,* Veggan thought, *maybe some excitement for a*

*change!* Code Seventy was a high-level defection. He took a pad and the stub of a pencil from his pocket. "Go ahead."

"Subjects are an older couple, married, late sixties. May use own papers, names, Dorst, Peter and Ruperta. Will be moving with a man, tall, dark hair, possibly West German agent."

"Got it," Veggan said. "Do they have transportation?"

"Yes, a staff car from motor pool. It's a black Volga M-124, plate number AR41-43."

Beads of sweat were popping out on the corporal's forehead and his hand holding the phone had started to shake.

He closed his eyes in concentration and conjured up the Volga he had seen in his single headlight at the cul-de-sac of Bidan Allee.

"Veggan, are you there? Do you copy?"

Slowly, so slowly the license plate became clear. He could see the numbers again . . . AR41-43.

"Veggan, damn you . . ."

"I am here, sir. The car is in my sector. I saw it just a few minutes ago."

"Where?"

"At the end of the cul-de-sac of Bidan Allee—"

"Get back there at once!"

"Yes, sir."

The line went dead and Veggan ran for the Volkswagen.

The helicopter was a small JU-12. It was only a two-seater, and since it was used primarily for Vopo surveillance work over the city, it was unarmed. For this reason, Negatov had already put an Mpik—the East German version of a Soviet AK-47 assault rifle—in the passenger seat along with three full, extra magazines.

The engine had warmed up and above him the rotors whirred lazily, ready for takeoff. He was about to hoist himself in, when he spotted Ziegler, the control communications officer, running toward him waving his arms in the air. Negatov dropped back to the apron when the man reached him almost too breathless to talk.

"Slow down, man, what is it?"

"The car, Herr Kapitän, it's been spotted!"

"The Volga, same license number?"

"Yes, sir, in a cul-de-sac on Bidan Allee, just beyond the fence around the old runway."

Negatov felt a twist in his gut as he grasped the man's shoulders. "Quickly, what's just inside the fence over there?"

"An old hanger. It's used as storage mostly, and a place for patrols on that perimeter. I've tried to call them for the last five minutes and there is no answer."

Negatov stared at the two sodium lamps nearly two miles away, and let his mind race. "Ziegler, are there any aircraft over there?"

"Yes. We park the short-range mail planes over there, an old Cherokee and a Stutz."

"Damn, that's it! Get three trucks of Vopos moving, one each to block both ends of the old runway, and send one directly to the hangar."

"Yes, sir, right away."

The man scurried away, and Negatov pulled himself into the chopper. "You heard?" The pilot nodded that he had. "Then move, as fast as possible!"

As the machine lifted off, Negatov levered a shell into the chamber of the assault rifle and clicked off the safety.

When the telephone rang, Carter almost answered it. His German was good enough and he thought he might be able to pass himself off as Zeisman. But, abruptly, just as he reached the instrument, the ringing stopped.

Quickly, he ran back inside the hangar. As quietly as possible he rolled the big door up after extinguishing the bench light. Grunting with the exertion, he rolled the Stutz out onto the apron by hand.

Then he was in the plane. He did a quick once-over of the controls with his penlight, set the gun on the number two seat, and fired up.

The engine caught, missed, and caught again, throwing blue exhaust smoke as it picked up revs. In seconds it settled down into the smooth, assured idle of a well-maintained engine.

The packs on the disc brakes squealed lightly as he turned the aircraft and taxied to the end of the apron. At the same time, he turned his head toward the darkness at the edge of the woods.

The Dorsts were running across the clear space beyond the fence as fast as their legs would carry them.

"Run!" Carter exhorted under his breath. "Run faster!"

Then he saw the uniformed Vopo. He was standing at the edge of the woods, shouting, his rifle raised to his shoulder.

The couple passed out of sight behind the gate as the Vopo fired. Carter grabbed the Beretta and vaulted from the plane. He hit the apron running, and was about twenty feet from the small door when it opened and the Dorsts burst through.

Peter Dorst was half carrying, half dragging his wife as he kicked the door closed. Two slugs slammed into it from the other side. He turned to Carter with tears streaming down his cheeks.

"Ruperta, she's hit."

Carter looked down where the woman's white face peeked from under her husband's arm. There were tears of pain in her eyes, but she was smiling.

"I . . . I think it is my back . . . somewhere."

"Can you get her to the plane?" Carter rasped.

"I think so."

"Then move!"

Carter dropped to one knee. He lifted the makeshift Beretta in both hands to the firing position and waited. Behind him, he could hear the old man's dragging footsteps and his heavy breathing.

The door in the gate slammed open and the Vopo lurched through. All his concentration was on the plane and the fleeing couple. He didn't even see Carter until the Killmaster fired, twice.

Both 9mm slugs hit him center chest. The Vopo dropped his rifle and fell back through the door.

Carter sprinted to the plane.

Dorst was struggling, trying to lift his wife up and through the small door. As gently yet as swiftly as possible, Carter got his arms under her and brought her up and into the rear seat. Then he hefted the old man in behind her.

"You'll have to take care of her yourself. I have to fly."

"I understand."

"Here's a light," Carter said. "There is a first aid kit there, in the pocket. The main thing is to stop the bleeding."

He slammed the door and scrambled over the console into the number one seat.

He kicked the revs up and released the brakes at the same time. The Stutz lurched forward.

In the distance, coming from the main terminal area across the main runways, he could see a helicopter coming their way in the air and the lights of a heavy vehicle on the ground.

He upped the revs and turned onto the old, rutted taxiway.

*Cool,* he thought, *be cool*. He kept one eye ahead and

one eye on the instruments going through a checklist as he sensed the helicopter's dancing spotlight heading right for the hangar.

The pitch was fine as he ran the power up to 1700 rpm. All the instruments were in normal ranges. Magneto drop was 125 rpm. Carburetor was applying heat, good suction pressure with a normal rpm drop.

He put the prop through a cycle from fine through coarse pitch back to fine, and it sounded gutsy.

The gyros were set and the altimeter read sea level.

He flipped the boost pump to on and gave it ten degrees flap. Out the window he could see the flaps cycling down. He left the navigational and strobe lights off.

With any luck the helicopter and truck wouldn't see him in the darkness, and wouldn't hear him over the roar of their own engines.

Then he saw the truck, Vopos already pouring off its flat bed. There were orange flashes everywhere as they hit the ground and fanned out. A slug hit the Plexiglas and careened away. Another came right on through and slammed into the radio box above Carter's head.

He hit the rudders and swung the little plane in a 180-degree turn on the runup pad until the nose was aligned to the center line.

"How are we?" he shouted over his shoulder.

"I don't know," Dorst answered. "I think I have stopped the bleeding. She has passed out."

"Well, buckle her up, and yourself," Carter said. "Ten minutes from now and we're home."

He didn't add, *if they don't blow us to hell first*.

He lowered the flaps to their limits and put them back to their trailing position. He fine-pitched the prop, and the Stutz, pinioned by the brakes, seemed to crouch on its nose gear, waiting to leap.

In the side mirror Carter could see the orange flashes getting closer, and he could hear the pings as the slugs slammed into the plane.

He hit the throttle and released the brakes.

Half.

Three-quarters.

Full.

From the cockpit the movement of the center line stripe became a blur and then a solid strip of faded white.

"Seventy knots, seventy-five . . . c'mon, baby!"

And then he saw them, two trucks, twin pairs of headlights coming down the runway straight at them.

There was little doubt as to their intent. If bullets wouldn't stop the little plane, then trucks would. They meant to hit him on each side with the heavy vehicles and rip the slender wings right off the plane's body.

"Dorst . . . ?"

"Yes, I see them."

"Hold your wife steady and do the best you can yourself. I'm going over the grass median to the main runway."

The words were scarcely out of Carter's mouth when his feet hit the rudders. The plane veered right and they were in the pulpy mush of the median.

The tires bogged, but between speed and lift they managed to slog through. Carter bit his lip and held the throttle at full.

He only hoped that there were no drainage ditches. If there were, the plane would nose over, probably flip, and it was all over.

The two trucks had veered with him. Now they were also on the median, but their tremendous weight was bogging them down to a crawl.

At last there was a final bump and they were on the main runway. Again Carter found the center line and in no time he got airspeed.

"One of the trucks is stuck!" Dorst called from the rear seat. "The other is on the runway but falling behind!"

"Good," Carter said, and pulled back on the wheel.

Then they had liftoff and the runway fell away. The landing gear hesitated but eventually lifted up into the belly.

Carter settled the airspeed for a fractional rate of climb, trimmed out the control pressures, and checked his oil.

The heat gauge was popping the red and climbing.

The hell with it, he thought, and didn't bother easing back the rpm. It was a twenty-mile flight. If the engine blew on the way down, then let it blow.

Visibility was nearly unlimited and the air was calm in the cloudless night. Calm except for the banshee whooshing as it came through the hole made by the bullet.

Off to their right was West Berlin. Carter put the Stutz into a rolling bank and nearly collided with the helicopter as it came up from beneath them.

"Jesus . . ."

"Willi, look out!" Dorst wailed.

The side door of the chopper was open. The machine was so close that Carter could make out the shooter's features in the panel lights as he let go with the assault rifle.

The slugs stitched across the Plexiglas, and Carter felt a tug at his right shoulder and then burning pain.

From behind him there was a gargled gasp but he didn't have time to investigate. He put the plane into a roll that it wasn't designed to make, and came up under and behind the helicopter.

The engine was still screaming, but the heat gauge was clear through the red.

Much longer like this and it would lock up.

As Carter had hoped, the helicopter pilot was savvy. He waited until Carter came out of the loop and then took the

Killmaster's dare. He dropped in right beside them and tilted his nose forward to match the Stutz's speed. In the open hatchway, Carter could see the second man jamming a new magazine into the rifle.

Keeping the Stutz steady with his knees, Carter opened the vent window. Leaning far back, he held the Beretta out the window in his right hand, with a fresh clip in his left.

The other man was just lifting the rifle when Carter fired until the clip was empty.

He knew he had a hit when the rifle lifted, the orange flashes going harmlessly into the sky.

Carter rammed home the new clip and started firing again. This time he sprayed the slugs all along inside the chopper.

The chopper pilot didn't take two seconds with slugs flying around the inside of his canopy. He veered away and Carter banked enough to head straight for the Wall.

There was machine-gun fire from the turrets lining the Wall, but at two thousand feet they were a skimpy target.

Then they were over. He banked right and headed for the lights of Templehof. He dropped to five hundred feet and started his glide.

Suddenly there was a choking sound from the engine and it started to sputter.

"Hang on, baby," he urged, "two more minutes."

He cut back the throttle and dropped the landing gear. It groaned and clanked but finally dropped into place and locked.

The runway was coming up fast. In the distance Carter could see the red and blue lights of fire trucks heading for the end of the runway. The tower would be alerted that there was a renegade, so there would be no other traffic to contend with.

He was down to final approach, still coming in too low

but not wanting to risk any further overheat of the engine.

100 feet.

50 feet.

The Stutz nosed down in a long glide pattern. Carter could see the shadow of descent from the ground lights. He inched forward in the seat, his hips straining against the belt.

The plane touched down and bounced slightly.

And then the overheat hit. There was a grinding sound and the pistons locked slightly. A second later the prop froze, causing a side swerve.

Carter did his best to correct as the wheels banged down again, jarringly. The jolt threw him forward. His head slammed against the Plexiglas, and almost at once he could feel blood running into his eyes.

Now it was all by feel. He could hardly see the end of the runway coming up and the fence beyond. He knew his speed was too great but he had no prop-thrust in reverse to cut it down.

He waited until the last possible minute before he stood on the brakes.

They screamed as the discs locked, and then flames shot out from beneath the plane when the pads wore through and it was steel against steel.

The nose swerved wildly. Carter moved his feet from the brakes to the rudder. He veered from side to side on the runway, trying to reduce speed.

Then they were off the runway, skidding on the grassy median. The right wingtip hit a light stanchion. The wing buckled, but not before the plane had been spun around.

A tire blew and the left wing hit the ground. Again Carter was head-slammed, this time against the heavy side brace.

The world was going black and foggy. . . .

He was floating.

And then he felt an agonizing pain where his right arm was being clutched by an overanxious hand.

The pain brought consciousness. He snapped his eyes open and looked up into a white, worried face topped by a wide-billed fireman's hat.

"Hey, this one's alive!"

"The old man," Carter groaned, "and the woman . . ."

"Sorry, they didn't make it."

Carter said one word—"Shit"—before he passed out.

# TEN

Senator Paul Colber lay on the aft sun deck of the yacht. He was naked and his body, at forty-three, was trim and bronzed from the sun.

He heard the anchor drop, hold, and seconds later the yacht swung around with the tide. When the slack was taken up in the anchor chain, the big boat began to rock lazily.

Colber was on his belly. He opened one eye and, four miles away, he saw the gleaming villas of St. Tropez glistening in the Mediterranean sun.

*The life,* he thought, *this is the life.* If his constituents could see him now, he would probably face a recall. If his wife could see him, she would have his balls in the oven.

A pity he had ever married, he mused. But it was hard to get elected without the family image. And then there was the money. Small-town lawyers didn't get elected to the U.S. Senate without money and connections. The woman he had chosen to marry twenty-eight years earlier had both.

Something about marriage, he thought, made men and women cease to become pleasure-seeking animals. Such was his own case, until a year before when he had met a woman in New York who had reignited those pleasure-seeking desires.

He felt the warm, gentle Mediterranean sun bathe his bare body. The yacht bobbed gently up and down in the water. Below, he could hear the four-man crew going about their duties. They would never come up on the sun deck unless they were summoned.

They were well trained and well paid by the yacht's owner, their beautiful mistress, to be discreet.

"More oil, darling?" she said. "You're drying out."

"Please," Colber sighed, and felt her fingers and palms working the sunscreen over his naked flesh. She oiled his shoulders, his back, his buttocks, and the backs of his legs down to the ankles.

"Good?"

"Hmmm."

"Turn over."

He turned. For a few seconds the sun blinded him. He shielded his eyes with a forearm and she came into focus. She, too, was naked, her body bronzed from the tops of her feet to her blond hair. Her body already glistened with oil as she leaned forward over him on her knees.

Her small, firm, dark-nippled breasts wavered above his eye. Her flat stomach and the dark triangle at its base wavered inches from his lips.

"You're getting new ideas," she smiled.

"I never gave up the old ones," he countered.

Her fingers worked more suntan lotion into his chest and glided downward. The palms kneaded his flat, spare stomach and passed over his groin to pay close attention to his legs and hips.

"Must you go this afternoon?"

"I must, and you know it," he sighed. "I have a meeting in Geneva tomorrow morning and it's important."

"Arms talks," she pouted, "always silly arms talks."

Her fingers began to tickle the inside of his thighs. It was a magic that always worked. He could feel blood rushing to his groin.

"Always the best forecast," she chuckled.

He moaned low in his throat, becoming languorous and almost semiconscious under her ministrations, floating in the pleasure her fingers brought him.

He listened to her voice and, without thinking, mumbled answers to her seemingly innocuous questions.

"What can be so important to the negotiators that you must be there yourself?"

"It is always a delicate situation when you give in on certain points." His own voice seemed to float somewhere above them both. Her magic fingers had lifted him to a euphoric state.

"But surely some aide could tell your people in Geneva what is to be given up to the Soviets?"

"That's not the point."

"Then what is?" She ran her fingers like a velvet comb through his pubic hair, bringing a gasp to his lips.

"It's a very delicate situation. We are prepared to agree on their last initiative, but it must be delivered in such a way that they think they must give up another point or two before we will accede."

"But if you are going to give them what they want, why not just tell them?"

He smiled at her naîveté. "Because there is always the chance that we can squeeze just a little more out of them before we say yes."

His eyes were closed. He didn't see the smile that curved

her sensuous lips and the narrowness of her eyes as she weighed her position.

Should she try to glean more? Or would she be satisfied with this?

She decided on the latter. They had told her to find out Washington's position on the last offer, and she had done just that. Further questioning and even this love-starved fool might question the questioning.

It was time to give Senator Colber his reward.

It meant little to her. Long ago it had become pointless to try and remember all the men she'd had and the number of times they had made love to her. Only a few were memorable.

Physical satisfaction was an easy thing for her. She could get it from any of them. She took it and accepted it as a normal reflex of her body. It meant little, and it brought them further under her spell.

The female orgasm.

It bolstered their egos so much when they knew they were the cause of it. It was just a convenience; she never had to fake it.

Her fingers reached his sex. She played with him, gently, knowingly, and he responded like a youth.

"Oh, my," she sighed, not needing to feign the pleasure in her voice.

He opened his eyes to see her wide blue eyes gazing back at him in innocence.

God, he thought, how superbly beautiful she was. She was one of those rare creatures endowed with blond hair and blue eyes whose skin could be tanned golden by the sun. She never burned or turned a lobster color.

"If I have you for just this afternoon," she told him, "then I shall take so much of you that there will be nothing left for another woman until I see you again."

"There is no other woman," he growled.

He curled his fingers around her neck beneath her hair and tugged her down. She came willingly, stretching her body full length over his. Their oiled flesh slid together. When her lips found his, he cupped her buttocks and ground himself against her.

"I'm ready for you," she said softly, very softly, against his ear. She knew he liked to feel her breath there, it excited him.

His penetration made them both gasp.

She settled over him, her face a mask of concentration on what was happening to her body. She pressed her knees into his ribs and leaned over him, palms flat against his heaving chest as he thrust harder and deeper inside her.

"Yes, hurt me, fill me," she hissed, rubbing her oil-slick buttocks against his legs.

Beneath them the yacht bobbed up and down in the water, moving with the rhythm of their bodies.

Her breathing became raspy. Before her slitted eyes, the shore, four miles away, rose and fell. It undulated with their liquid movements.

She gritted her teeth and tightened her thighs. He gasped and bucked upward harder until their bones ground against each other.

"Yes, yes!" she cried, looking down into his face. It was twisted and contorted with almost unbearable pleasure.

"Now!" she groaned.

He nodded frantically.

The rhythm of her hips became like the pulsating piston of a high-speed engine. And from her lips spewed words of filth in three languages. There was no end to her range. Verbally she abused him, calling up the languages of the gutters of a hundred cities.

It made him wild.

The intensity of his lust freed her own. She cried out. The shock waves rippled through her groin, her belly, and made her breasts ache.

She felt him explode and tightened her hold on him until the contractions ceased. Then the warm, weak limpness came, and she fell over him.

They lay embraced, smelling the heady mix of their bodies with the salt sea air.

But not for long.

They never relaxed for long after their lovemaking. It often bothered him, but he accepted it as part of her nature. It was as though her desire was on tap—she turned it on and off at will. And afterward she was always brusque, as if to get on with something else.

"Hurry now," she said, "we can't have you missing your plane."

Colber complied, feeling oddly empty.

He was no longer in her mind. Already she was hurrying through the night to Major Sergei Kostovich, so she could pass on what she had learned and get it over with.

As she showered the oil and Colber from her body, she remembered the last time with Sergei. It has been the only time for years that she had made love for the sake of making love.

She had actually felt and enjoyed it, mentally as well as physically.

Idly, she thought that maybe, just maybe, she would enjoy it again with Sergei.

The thought of this brought another: Was she actually finding the life she had wanted so much now growing bitter?

# ELEVEN

When Carter opened one eye, the sun winked at him through a large window. The sun hurt. He closed his eye. A few seconds passed and he tried again, this time in response to a sound from somewhere in the room. He didn't move his head, just the pupil of one eye, until he saw her.

She was very pretty, around thirty, give or take a year. She was puttering at a tray.

"Water," he groaned.

She turned, surprise on her face. Quickly she poured water from a pitcher into a glass and moved toward the bed. As she got nearer, the foggy aura disappeared around her.

Her face, without makeup, was striking, and what he could see of her shape wasn't bad at all. She was wearing a tailored white dress that didn't exactly put her on display, but he could see that her legs were shapely from ankles to knees, plump at the calves, and just the right width at the hips.

She held his head while he drank thirstily.

"Where am I?" he said, when she removed the glass from his lips.

"A safe house near the Havel. You spent one night in the hospital, but when they learned that agents had come over from the East to find you, they moved you here."

"Who are you?"

"Gerta. I am a nurse." She laid his head back and plumped the pillows. The movement tightened her bodice, revealing two very large breasts. "How are you feeling?"

"Like hell. What was the damage?"

"A fairly serious concussion, a fairly small wound in your right thigh, and a slightly more serious one in your upper right arm. You also broke the little finger on your right hand. You will live."

Carter watched her move back to the tray. In the starchy uniform she had a beautiful behind.

He told her so. "You have a beautiful behind."

She smiled over her shoulder. "Now I know you will live. Are you hungry?"

There was no answer. Carter had already slipped back to sleep.

She was still there when he woke up again, only the white uniform had been replaced by a skirt and sweater. She sat in an easy chair polishing her nails.

She looked even better this time than the last. Dark red lipstick, some rouge, and a little eye makeup had been added. The red sweater clung loosely to the swelling outline of her breasts. Her hair lay in careless swirls about her head and coiled down around her shoulders. The swaying motion of her breasts when she rubbed the buffer across her nails fascinated him.

He told her so.

She threw back her head and laughed. "Are all Americans like you?"

"I certainly hope not."

She dropped the buffer into her purse and stood. "Are you up to dictating a report?"

"I suppose so, as soon as I've had a steak. How long have I been out?"

"Four days. I'll telephone your people."

The steak was rare, over an inch thick, with boiled potatoes and two vegetables. The wine was a good French red, and Carter enjoyed watching her cut his meat almost as much as he did eating it.

"Are you on a twenty-four-hour shift?"

She nodded. "The fewer people who know where you are right now, the better."

He was drinking coffee when Marty Jacobs from the Berlin AXE office sauntered into the room.

"My man, you are indestructible!"

"So they tell me," Carter said, grinning. "What's happening in the world? Or, rather, what happened?"

Jacobs spoke as he pulled a small tape recorder, a pad, and a batch of pencils from his briefcase. He looked more like a CPA on his night off than a crack AXE agent. He had an owlish face and a lean body with long, ropey muscles in a short-sleeved shirt and a pair of faded jeans. Aviator glasses spanned his eyes and covered his cheekbones, emphasizing his wise-owl look.

"You raised hell on the way over. Two dead, and a few banged up bad. One was a Vopo corporal. The one in the helicopter was a hot shot, a captain. His name was Igor Negatov."

Carter smiled. It hurt his face. "I tried to get the helicopter too."

"I know. From what we can learn, you barely missed. In short, you are on their shit list. They have all their locals on this side turning West Berlin inside out trying to find you."

"Good."

"We've leaked that you're already back in the States."

The smile dropped from Carter's face. "How did the Dorsts get it?"

"Quick," Jacobs said, pulling a chair close to the bed and setting up his gear. "They took about five slugs each in the upper body. You were lucky."

"That was the bastard in the chopper," Carter growled. "What about Weist and Mueller?"

"Disappeared. You know what that means."

Carter nodded, the steak turning to lead in his gut. "So they got all four of them. Double X is dead."

"That's the size of it. Want to talk?"

Carter nodded. "Gimme a cigarette."

"They said you shouldn't smoke."

"Bullshit."

"Right."

Jacobs lit him a cigarette and Carter talked. He relayed every detail of every conversation and every move he had made while he was in the East. He parroted back Peter Dorst's comments and theories about how they had been betrayed, and added his own thoughts.

He talked for almost two hours, until his eyes started to close.

"Well," Jacobs said at last, "not much doubt of it. Looks like the leak was on our side. What about this Este?"

"No chance," Carter replied, slurring his words.

"You're sure?"

"Damn sure. He knows I would kill him. He likes living."

Jacobs stood. "I'll be back in the morning. I imagine Washington will want you quiet and out of the way for a few more days. I'll let you know."

"Do that."

The body beautiful came in as Jacobs went out. She had a small plate and a glass of milk. On the plate was a pill.

"What's that?"

"A sleeping pill."

"Believe me, I don't need it."

His eyes were already at half-mast. By the time she hit the door again they had fallen all the way.

The dreams, bad dreams, started right away. He saw the old man and the old woman running. He saw the frail white face, teary-eyed, staring at him from under her husband's arm. He saw the old dentist's face smiling down at him, and imagined what they had done to him to get him to talk.

He woke up screaming. Gerta was holding him down. He was wringing wet.

"You were having a nightmare."

"I know. I'll take that pill after all."

Jacobs came back the next afternoon to clear up some odds and ends.

"Hawk will be in touch," he said when leaving.

It was two days later when Hawk called.

"How are you feeling?"

"Better, almost good."

"We're putting a lot of ends together here. We should have something concrete in four or five days. When we do—"

"I want it," Carter growled.

"Good enough. Stay quiet until then. BfV says the house and nurse are ours until you don't need them anymore."

"I think I'll move on. You can get me at Berlin 755-418."

"You're sure?"

"I'm sure. I found out my nurse is married."

•   •   •

Carter knew where he was going, where he was going to hole up for a few days and nights, but first he decided to exorcise his demons.

Only once before in his long career had he let death get to him. That had been an old woman, too, in Spain. Now he had the demon of an old man and an old woman to get rid of. And a dentist. And a man named Dieter Weist he hadn't even met.

The "sin strip" along the lower end of the Kurfürstendamm was perfect for his mood.

He walked through the pimps and whores and hawkers, and hoped one or more of the young toughs who eyed his expensive suit would try him on.

A garish row of neons in a narrow alley off the Ku-damm drew him. Short-skirted women lined the doorways on both sides of the street. One, all legs and bust, whispered to him of the many apertures she was willing to place at his disposal for the paltry sum of thirty marks.

He chose a subterranean sleaze palace called The Joker, and went down into its dim bowels.

The place was jammed. A ten-mark note passed to a maître d' in a tacky tuxedo did wonders. Miraculously, over the heads of the audience, a tiny table was passed from one waiter to another until it was deposited at the very edge of a small stage.

Would mein Herr step this way?

Mein Herr would, and ordered Niersteiner and a bottle of brandy. Mein Herr was embarking on an epic drunk.

He was on his second glass when a baby-blue spot skewered a beam of light to the center of the stage. A hearty but bad three-piece combo flailed out a downbeat. The curtains at the rear of the stage parted and—according to a voice from backstage—Mademoiselle Fifi, direct from Paris, stepped into the spot.

Mademoiselle Fifi was about six-five in five-inch heels, and minced out in a gold lamé dress that had seen better days years before and had one hell of a time containing its contents.

Ten seconds into the routine and she began peeling off her gloves. Twenty seconds into the routine and the banana-skin dress joined the gloves on a chair.

Beneath it was a lacy teddy that had also seen better days. The teddy was as tight on her body as the dress had been.

Carter let his eyes run down over her neck and shoulders. They dwelt on her ample bosom and slid down the hourglass waist to the flaring fullness of hips and thighs.

"An Amazon!" someone called from the audience.

"The backside of a brood mare," hooted another.

"Shhh!" hissed a third.

Carter drank and held up his glass for another bottle of brandy. Mademoiselle Fifi was doing nothing for him.

Either she spotted the man in the expensive suit or the maître d' had tipped her off about his good tip. In any event, she moved Carter's way and started playing directly to him.

Slowly she turned to give him the full view—the firm outline of the buttocks, almost shining through the satin teddy. Her every movement was studied and voluptuous. Then, making sure she had his attention, she reached for the ends of a ribbon bow and started to unlace the bodice from cleavage to crotch. In a single movement the teddy fell to the floor.

Under the teddy?

Nothing. *Nada*. Not a damn thing.

Carter poured the last of the second bottle of Niersteiner into his glass, and added a lot of brandy.

Then she began to dance to a lazy Latin rhythm which, almost imperceptibly, began to accelerate. As the music upped its tempo, Fifi matched it with her movements. Eventually everything was shaking like a gigantic Jell-O mold. At last, glistening from the exertion, Fifi fell back in the chair and grabbed her ankles. Her legs went high in the air and equally as wide.

The spotlight flipped off and the patrons went wild.

Carter held up his glass for a third bottle of Niersteiner.

About five minutes later, Mademoiselle Fifi slid into the chair beside him and squeezed his leg.

"You like my dance?"

"You were great," Carter said.

"You are American?"

"Russian," he replied, slurring his accented German even harder with a Slavic accent.

"Oh."

She looked like the bottom had fallen out of her teddy, but came around to the fact that he still looked like the best prospect for between-the-shows profit.

"You buy Fifi a drink?"

"Sure."

Carter paid ten marks for a glass of colored water, toasted her, and drank his Niersteiner and brandy.

It was having the desired effect.

Girls, all shapes, all sizes, had erupted from somewhere. Most of them were dressed like Fifi, and all of them had managed to lure a customer from his table to dance on the stage.

The stage became a sea of grinding loins before Carter's watery eyes. Some of the girls wore skirts split to their waists. The splits were open and there was nothing under the skirts.

It was a surrealistic dream, a sight to dazzle the beholder, even the sober beholder, and Carter was drunk.

"You wish to dance?" Fifi asked.

"No," Carter replied.

"We can be much closer on the stage, dancing."

"I can see that," he replied.

Her hand went from his thigh to his crotch. "I have a room upstairs, very nice, very quiet."

"No, thanks."

"Only a hundred marks."

Carter turned his head to face her. "Mademoiselle, if I were looking to rent a Mercedes, I wouldn't shop for it in a place where they rent only used Volkswagens."

The colored water hit him squarely in the face.

"You are a swine!" she hissed, and stood. "You cannot insult Fifi this way!"

Carter saluted her with the last of his brandy as she stalked away.

He waited five minutes and hit the street. The fresh air was heaven after the smoky interior. He took time to light a cigarette a few steps down the alley, and saw the black leather jacket slip out of the door of the club and stand, watching him.

He was big, with burly shoulders and loglike arms in the sleeves of the leather jacket.

That was good, Carter thought. It wouldn't do if he was small.

Carter chose the dark end of the alley and headed for it, whistling. It took about a half block for Leather Jacket to catch up and fall in step with him.

"Excuse me, mein Herr."

"*Ja?*" Carter said, staggering slightly, keeping his eyes front.

"My name is Bernau."

"That's nice."

"Here, on the Ku'-damm, they call me Bernau the Black."

"Is that right."

"I do not like foreigners to insult my girls, mein Herr. It is not good for my business, and it gives me . . . how do you say . . . a bad image."

Carter stopped, the smoke from the cigarette in his lips curling up over his hooded eyes. They turned at once to face each other.

"Image? My image of you, Bernau, is that of a punk who smells, dresses in jeans, and needs a shave."

Bernau's broad, flat-nosed face broke into a smile.

"Mein Herr, I was only going to charge you fifty marks for insulting my woman. Now you have insulted me as well. That will cost you one hundred marks."

"Fair enough," Carter said. "It was the figure I had in mind."

The Killmaster held out his hand and opened it. Inside it were two fifty-mark notes.

Bernau smiled and swaggered forward. He reached for the bills and Carter grasped his wrist. At the same time, he dropped to one knee and swung. Bernau sailed by him and crashed, headfirst, into the brick wall.

He whirled, blood pouring from his nose, and roared like a wounded animal.

"Come, Bernau," Carter said smoothly, "come here so I can shove the money up your ass."

He came like a runaway truck, big arms flailing, knees high, trying to find Carter's groin.

Carter played. He sidestepped, backed off, and came in again. All the time he danced, he hit; a left, a right, two lefts, two rights.

Bernau's head was on a pendulum, back and forth.

When the man's face was hamburger, Carter backed off and gave his hands a rest. Instead, as Bernau came again, he used his feet—to the shin, to the knees, to the gut.

But Bernau took it and kept coming in for more. His

bloody face was a mixture of fear and hate, but he was too stupid to know when to quit.

Carter backed to a wall and dropped his hands in invitation. Bernau locked his own fists and swung heavily. He missed his dodging opponent by a good eight inches and smashed his hands into the wall.

He cried out in pain and whirled. His eyes were wild with pain and rage, but he could hardly find the Killmaster's darting figure.

"Over here, punk, right over here."

"You bastard!" he howled, hurling his bull-like body at Carter.

They slammed to the ground, Carter rolling out from under even as they hit, regaining his feet and crouching as Bernau came at him again. It was like a steer hurtling toward a dancing matador as Bernau's impetus brought him closer and closer to the speeding fist of his opponent.

The collision was all one way, blood spurting out of Bernau's mouth as bone and flesh met his face at devastating velocity. He sailed backward, careening onto and over a trash can. He came to rest, belly up, in a puddle.

Carter knelt beside him and slipped the two fifty-mark bills into his breast pocket.

"Thank you, Bernau the Black. Thank you very much. You're better than a shrink."

And then he walked on down the alley, whistling.

# TWELVE

"Erica the Red," Carter said.

"What?"

"Nothing. I was just musing. Erica the Red is even better therapy than Bernau the Black."

"What in God's name does that mean?" Erica von Falkener asked, her green eyes flashing across the candlelit table.

"It means," he replied, "that you are beautiful and I'm glad I came running to you in my hour of need."

She shook her head and, with a smile, speared a meatball.

Carter did the same.

It had been three days since he had shown up at her apartment door with drunken, watery eyes, wounds, and bruised, bleeding knuckles.

"You look like hell," she had said, her lips parted, a curl of red hair straying over her right eye.

"I feel wonderful."

"You need a bed."

"That I do."

She had trundled him into the bedroom, undressed him, and poured him between the sheets. By the time she had killed the lights and slipped in beside him, he was sound asleep.

Not so the next morning.

When Carter had opened his eyes, the sun winked at him through the window. He moved. Surprisingly, his body didn't ache as much as he'd expected.

He closed his eyes again and yielded to the sensations Erica's body offered. She lay on her back beside him, her round behind nestled tightly against his thigh. The scent of her teased his nostrils.

She lay still and let him gaze down at her. A soft smile made her lips twitch.

"I hope," she murmured, "that you're thinking what I think you're thinking."

"Coffee."

"What?"

"I'm thinking about coffee."

She rubbed her bare buttocks against his leg and let her hands roam over his body. After a few moments she purred deep in her throat.

"Still coffee?"

"Among other things," he chuckled.

"Ummmm." She turned over slowly and threw an arm around his shoulder and pulled him close. His breathing roared in her ear, and when she felt him stir between her thighs, she pressed herself tightly against him. "I always eat breakfast," she said. "It's the most important meal of the day."

There was something exquisite about making love early in the morning, while the senses were still half asleep. It was slower, more dreamlike. The smells were headier. The sensations seemed to ooze and float, and it was all so liquid.

When the final tremors of orgasm died away, she said softly, "We're quite good together, I think."

"Yes," he answered.

He lay on his back and stared blankly at the ceiling, which had a few cracks. His palm lay gently on one of her breasts; he rubbed it idly.

"We could be so much better."

She was right. In the times they'd been together, he felt as though he could not leave her without a feeling of emptiness. His tongue felt thick in his throat. So he just nodded a couple of times.

But no matter the gulf they both knew lay between them, they didn't stir from the apartment. For different reasons, they hadn't been able to get enough of each other. And it had gone on for the next three days.

Eventually Erica had asked, and Carter had told her, not all of it, just enough to let her know that it had been bad.

Earlier that evening he had sensed that the time was drawing near. The call was coming. He had suggested a night on the town and she had agreed.

"Do you like them?" she asked, gesturing toward his plate.

"Delicious . . . for meatballs."

"Ah," she laughed, "they are more than just meatballs. They are *Konigsberger Klops,* named for that city in East Prussia. A whole lemon and the black peppercorns give them the distinctively tart taste."

Carter almost said that the town of Konigsberger was now controlled by the Soviets and called Kaleningrad, but her enthusiasm made him hold his tongue.

They ate and drank in silence for several moments. When Erica spoke again, it was with a wistful sigh.

"When will you be going to the opera again?"

Carter's gut tightened, but he made no outward display of it. He also evaded the question. "When will you be going husband-hunting again?"

It broke the spell. She laughed. "No more, I'm afraid. There's no need, really. My investments have made me quite independent, actually."

"Good."

She came back to it. "Do spies ever retire?"

"I never said I was a spy."

"You never had to."

Carter thought for a moment. "I hate to disappoint you, but in answer to your question, no, they rarely retire."

"Why?" Her eyes were very serious now, more serious than Carter wanted to see them.

"Why what?"

"Why do you care if you disappoint me?"

"Because you are very nice, very beautiful, and I enjoy being with you, and the food is superb. I like you a great deal, even though I don't really know you."

"Nor I you."

Carter shrugged a shoulder and took a sip of wine.

After leaving the restaurant, they walked, holding hands, into the Berlin night. He put his arm around her waist and she snuggled tightly against his side. His fingers felt soft, yielding flesh beneath her clothes.

"Berlin is a lovely city," he said.

"A nice place to visit but you wouldn't want to live here."

They walked the rest of the way to her apartment in silence.

They were just inside the apartment when the phone started ringing. With a quick, gloomy glance at Carter, Erica answered it.

*"Ja?"* She listened for a few seconds and then held the phone out to him. "It's for the American gentleman."

Carter took it and she disappeared into the bedroom.

"Yes?"

"How is the weather there?"

"Balmy," Carter replied, "but there's a threat of rain."

"Then you probably won't mind moving south."

"Not at all."

"Mr. Pause would like to meet you tomorrow evening."

"Fine," Carter said. "Tell D.F. that I can make it around seven."

"Seven will be perfect. The corporate apartment?"

"I still have the key," Carter said, and the line went dead.

D. F. Pause was the field name for David Hawk, head of AXE. If Hawk himself was coming over for the briefing, they had something hot and concrete.

"Time to go?"

He looked up. Erica had changed into a negligee, sheer and almost the color of her skin.

He nodded.

"Well," she said with a sad smile, "it sure was fun."

"Fun's not over," Carter replied. "My plane doesn't leave until a little after ten in the morning."

She beat him to the bed.

He bought a carry-on bag on the way to the airport, and filled it with odds and ends of spare clothing and toiletries. It seemed that he was always traveling light, buying along the way. He wondered how many wardrobes he had left strewn around the world over the years.

They started boarding shortly after Carter arrived. He checked the bag, used his diplomatic passport to get his tools—a 9mm Luger and a stiletto—on board, and walked onto the plane.

He managed to eat the awful breakfast during the short flight to Frankfurt. During the hour layover between planes, he moved around the Frankfurt terminal almost constantly. Twice he went so far as to actually leave the building and stroll through the parking lot.

As far as he could tell, no one paid particular attention to him.

He surprised himself by sleeping soundly on the flight to Paris. He had no guesses about the evening meeting, but he had already decided that he would take it as it came.

Carter nodded courteously as the customs officer waved him through. A second officer took the slip for his special permit and guided him into a small room where the Luger and the stiletto were handed over.

Paris was bathed in pale sunlight, but Carter was too immersed in his own thoughts to appreciate the grandeur. He instructed the driver to take him to a small pension in the Montmartre section, and settled back with the morning edition of the Paris *Herald Tribune*.

The pension was on a small, neat, quiet street made up of shops and outdoor cafés. He checked in and pàid three days in advance. In the room, he unpacked the small bag and then called the alert number in the Paris AXE office.

"Four-nine-three," came a woman's voice in clipped, barely accented English.

"Would you please inform Mr. Pause that his star salesman is in?"

"I will do that, monsieur. The meeting is set for the same time."

"I'll be arriving early, as usual," Carter replied, and hung up.

He showered, shaved, and changed clothes. Beneath his shirt he attached Hugo's chamois sheath. The Luger went under his left armpit in a thin but sturdy shoulder rig.

At the door, he took a last look at the room. There was nothing that said its occupant would not be back in a few hours. Of course he would not return to the room at all, not even for the bag and its meager contents.

In the street, he hailed a cab to the Place Vendôme. It

was midafternoon and the crowds were heavy. Beautiful, well-dressed women laden with packages moved with the pedestrian traffic at a leisurely pace. Men sauntered, enjoying the day and the women.

Standing on a corner, taking his time lighting a cigarette, Carter, without seeming to, squinted his eyes to pick out another's faltering step or furtive glance.

Seeing none, he turned into the Rue de Rivoli and strolled down to the Place de la Concorde. Then he angled off into the maze of little back streets between Rue de Faubourg-St. Honoré and Boulevard Malesherbes.

At the juncture of Avenue de Friedland and Boulevard Haussmann, where the posh modern art galleries snared the tourists, he found a café and ordered a leisurely lunch.

All through the meal he watched the street and his neighboring diners.

Nothing.

After a brandy and coffee, he headed for the Champs-Elysées where he picked up his pace. On the other side of the Arc de Triomphe, he turned onto the Avenue de la Grande Armée, and hailed another cab.

"Gare St. Lazare," he said, and checked the rear window.

If anyone had been able to follow him through all that, he decided, more power to them.

The AXE apartment was in one of those charming old houses of graying stone with cypress trees in the front garden and a few hopeful daffodils that weren't doing too well.

He went up in the creaking elevator and opened the outer door with a master key that opened the same kind of locks in apartment doors all over the world. In the jamb between the outer and inner doors was a small panel. Behind the panel was a set of buttons. Carter dialed the correct code and entered the apartment.

In seconds an old woman waddled into the room. "Monsieur?'' she said, no surprise whatsoever on her face. If this stranger had the combination to enter the apartment, then he belonged.

*"Café et Calvados, s'il vous plaît."*

*"Oui, monsieur."*

She shuffled away and Carter checked his watch. It was five sharp. He knew that Hawk would arrive at precisely seven.

He would drink the coffee and the Calvados and force himself to wait calmly.

At two minutes past seven, David Hawk slid into a chair across from Carter and removed an inch-thick stack of neatly typed papers from his battered briefcase. Carefully, he spread them on the coffee table between them.

"We're not positive, but we have enough coincidences that we may have come up with a connection."

Here he paused to light the chewed stub of his cigar, and then launched into it.

"Through the years, only six people knew of the existence of Double X. Only two people knew the Dorsts' real names. The think-tank boys have taken each of these people apart and put them back together again."

Here Hawk spread out the papers in front of Carter until they became six dossiers.

"There is no need for you to go over all of them. We think they all have one thing in common."

"Which is?"

Hawk dived back into the briefcase and came up with another file folder. This one contained a thick biography and several eight-by-ten photographs.

Carter thumbed through the pictures first. They were all of a tall, aristocratic-looking woman with golden blond hair.

Her features were classic and her body was breathtakingly beautiful.

One photo in particular seemed to catch all of her. At first, Carter thought she was nude. Then he realized that the dress was flesh-colored, a shimmering single piece of silk that covered her from her neck to her slippered feet. It was molded to her breasts, flowed over a tiny waist and sharply swelling hips, then separated to cling like paint to her firm thighs and calves.

Carter glanced up. "Lotta woman."

Hawk made a grunting noise and clamped his teeth harder over the remnants of his cigar. "Olga Siskova. The 'Great Olga.' "

Carter looked back to the picture with narrowed eyes. "Yeah. I'm not much of an opera buff, but that rings a little bell."

"At five years of age she was a prodigy on the piano. As she grew older it was obvious that her crystal-clear soprano voice would bring her even more fame than her talented fingers. By the time she was nineteen, she was the toast of the entire Soviet bloc. On her twentieth birthday she charmed Moscow as well. But everything was not rosy . . . not for her, or for her Soviet managers and promoters."

"What do you mean?" Carter asked.

Hawk concentrated on a smoke ring that hovered about his head like a halo. "Olga Siskova was—and is—an amoral brat. Between twenty and thirty, her fame grew, and so did her temper. In short, she became a royal pain in the ass. No one could handle her. When they finally let her take an international tour outside the Soviet Union, she defected. It was generally believed at the time that the Russians let her go with a sigh of relief."

"I remember now," Carter said. "It was in Italy, Milan.

She refused to return to the company. She asked for, and got, political asylum.''

Hawk nodded. ''And she was not only an exquisite artist, she was also a flaming personality. She became the darling of the jet set. All doors were opened to her. She rarely sings anymore, but then she doesn't have to. She's fabulously wealthy, and what she doesn't have she can get just by asking for it.''

''Slowly it dawns,'' Carter growled. ''The pack she runs with could be talkers.''

''Exactly,'' Hawk said, nodding. ''After her defection she was outspoken in her tirades against Communism and the Soviet Union. She even wrote two books denouncing them. The books were best sellers, and made her the darling of conservatives all around the world.''

''And opened a lot of doors.''

''Speaking of doors,'' Hawk replied, ''one of the doors that was open a lot of the time, to the right people, was to her bedroom.''

He paused here and then, as he spoke again, pointed at the dossiers one by one.

''Charles Westlake, retired head of NATO security. Sir Thomas Ryder, retired chief of European intelligence analysis for MI6. Wolfgang Boesch, former head of West German internal security . . .''

''Her lovers?'' Carter asked.

''Every one of them. The other three are women who are very social on an international scale. They court Siskova as though she were a queen. We're still going through the guest lists for dinner parties and God knows what other functions where these women introduced Siskova to the very biggest guns in international business and politics.''

''You've gotten to them all?''

''Almost,'' Hawk replied, a cloud dropping over his face.

"We did it quietly, but not quietly enough. Wolfgang Boesch hung himself in his Bavarian chalet just before we got to him."

"And . . . ?"

"Boesch was the man who recruited and controlled Dieter Wiest."

"Damn," Carter hissed. "Is somebody on her now?"

"No," Hawk said. "We don't want to start anything we can't finish . . . at least not yet. But we might have a look-see. Senator Paul Colber spent a weekend with her at her villa on the Côte d'Azur. Right after that he went to the Geneva negotiations. Nick, the Russians were way ahead of him. It jarred him. He's a smart man. He smelled a rat and went back over everything. He himself came up with Olga Siskova, and was man enough to come to us with it. What he told us isn't enough to put a lid on her coffin, but it points us in the right direction."

"What now?"

Hawk stood. "Read what we've got on her. I've got a plan. It's got holes in it, but after you read that maybe we can play them and get going." He lumbered from the room to order a meal for them from the old cook.

Carter turned to the first page of the thick file and began to read.

# THIRTEEN

Olga Siskova learned very young, almost from the cradle, that the KGB was everywhere. While her teachers taught the glories of Soviet Socialist life, her parents taught her to have a discerning eye and a cautious tongue when speaking her thoughts.

Most of these thoughts were put into her developing mind by her discerning parents.

"Socialism is indeed the answer. But Communism? Bah!"

"Tyranny under the czar was leadership of the masses by one. Leadership under the Presidium is rule of the masses by a few. The Revolution changed the storekeepers, but it is still business as usual!"

Olga had an enormous talent and a keen, quick mind. By the age of ten, she began to realize the vagaries of what she was being taught. She saw that in the Soviet "classless" society there were indeed two classes: the peasant or near-peasant, and the "new class" or elitist society.

By that age she had also become accomplished at doublethink. She was able to absorb and spout back the party rhetoric she heard; she was also able to assess and understand all that was said during hushed conversations with her parents in their apartment or on outings in the countryside.

Her father, Petr: "Our way of life is ruled by just a few men, Olga. They have splendid apartments in Moscow and *dachas* on the Black Sea. Their every thought and action is geared to the preservation of their power."

Her mother, Natalia: "You must find a way to acquire party membership, Olga, and once that is done you must hone whatever skills you possess to rise in the party. It is not enough to be on the fringes: you must be on the inside."

And both of them together stressed that, as Olga grew older, she would see deprivation, cruelty, and injustice. To all these things she must close her eyes, because she could not change them. The only things that mattered were position and money. Once these two things were achieved, Olga could live her own life.

Shortly after she had applied to the Moscow Conservatory, they came . . . two men in long dark coats with stern faces.

"Petr Vasilevitch Siskov, you are accused of being an enemy of the people."

Amid the tears of his wife and daughter, Petr was taken away. It was never stated what Petr Siskov had done to become an "enemy of the people." For many months, Natalia tried to see her husband. She begged friends with party connections to intercede on her husband's behalf. Only too soon, Natalia found that she and Petr no longer had friends.

At the end of the year, both mother and daughter realized that it would be a long time before they saw Petr Vasilevitch again, if ever.

Outwardly, Olga learned to avert her eyes when asked about her father. She conditioned herself to be servile and declare in an embarrassed and ashamed tone, "My father is no longer a person; he is an enemy of the people."

But in her heart she knew that the state had struck a blow against her and her mother that she would never forgive.

Natalia had been a teacher of music and languages. Suddenly she was demoted. Even with Olga being a child genius and a protégée of great musicians, the state stepped in and the women were forced to move from the two-room apartment they had occupied alone to another two-room apartment they shared with another family.

This second deprivation only hardened the young girl's resolve to heed her father and mother's words. She perfected her foreign languages—French, German, Italian, and English—under her mother's tutelage. She studied Marxist-Leninist theory until she astounded her instructors with her knowledge and zeal.

And she turned to music with a vengeance. Long hours were spent with her music teachers. As her voice expanded, her body grew. It had long been apparent to her mother that Olga was an exceptionally talented and beautiful child. Now her instructors began noticing as well. Word was passed on.

By the summer of her sixteenth year, Olga was physically and emotionally a woman. Her body had blossomed to the point where male eyes followed every move. Long, graceful legs, flowing hips, and provocative breasts gave her a seductive quality far beyond her years. A full mane of blond hair and flashing blue eyes added to her allure.

To all those around her, Olga seemed perfect. Only the girl herself realized the one glaring flaw in her character. She was emotionless; she couldn't feel.

When she confided this to her mother, Natalia replied, "Perhaps this is good, my child. In our Soviet way of life, to feel is to hurt, to have heartaches. If you can live without emotion, you can live without pain. One who does not feel pain cannot be conquered."

Such bitterness had become common in her mother, and it made Olga resolve to succeed even more.

But when one's very life and breath is controlled by the state, success can be achieved only *through* the state.

For another year she studied. Twice she auditioned and took the exams that would place her in the conservatory and open the way for a career in grand opera. Both times she was refused. She was becoming convinced that her father's reputation would forever cast its shadow over her own life.

Then one day a man apeared at her door. His name was Yuri Kosyrev.

Kosyrev was listed on the conservatory staff as liaison officer between the main school in Moscow and its Minsk and Leningrad counterparts. But virtually all of his co-workers knew that Yuri Kosyrev was, in reality, a recruitor for the KGB.

"Olga, you have been accepted to the conservatory. But in view of your high grades and your . . . other talents, my superiors feel that there is even a higher area in which you could serve Mother Russia and our great socialist state."

"I am honored, Comrade Kosyrev."

It was the proper reply and delivered in a coldly impersonal manner that seemed to please the man.

"There will be a great deal of intensive training involved, and at its conclusion there may be risks."

"No risk is too great for the good of the state."

The dark pupils of Kosyrev's world-weary eyes studied Olga's beautiful face and attempted to plumb the depths of the emotionless blue eyes that stared vacantly back at him.

He couldn't, and it puzzled him. It also disturbed him. He felt that he was in the presence of someone who was not real, not complete, but totally in control. She had the appearance, she said the right things, and she had done the right things. There was no earthly reason why Yuri Kosyrev should not recruit her and recommend her.

Yet for some reason he found himself wanting to find one.

"There is the problem of your father . . ."

"Petr Vasilevitch is an enemy of the people. I have not seen him or heard from him in years."

The sudden chill in Kosyrev's hooded eyes told Olga that she had scored highly. There is nothing a KGB officer admires more than a child who is willing to turn in his or her own parent for the good of the state. Decrying her own father as an enemy of the state made Kosyrev see that, since her father's arrest, Natalia had raised her daughter in accord with the moral code of the builder of Communism.

"You will be informed, Comrade Siskova."

It was the end of the interview. As Olga closed the door behind the man, she allowed herself a slight smile. She hadn't meant or believed one word she had uttered, but she knew she had convinced Yuri Kosyrev of the opposite.

That evening she repeated the entire interview to her mother.

"My little one, from now on you must think only of yourself. Once you commit to those KGB bastards, you have but one path, upward mobility and survival. It is a dangerous choice, but one that will give you a better life than this. Take it if they offer, and from this day on think of only yourself."

Then, in the cold chill of a barren room, mother and daughter embraced. A solitary tear ran from Olga's eye.

It would be the last tear she would shed for many years.

Yuri Kosyrev himself escorted Olga Siskova to the conservatory. For two nights she was installed in an apartment not far from the Kremlin. It was lavishly appointed, with regal damask furniture, Oriental rugs, a kitchen, and a private bath. It was unlike anything the girl had ever seen.

The first night she scarcely slept. Her eyes refused to close as she lay alone in the huge double bed surveying the spendor of a bedroom bathed in the moonlight of a clear Moscow night.

It was the first bedroom Olga had ever seen that did not also serve as a living room, a sitting room, and a kitchen.

It was also the first time Olga had ever slept in a room without at least two other occupants.

"I have never seen such opulence," she exclaimed the next morning as she sipped tea made in a silver samovar and dabbed at her lips with a real linen napkin.

Yuri Kosyrev smiled and gave her hand a friendly, reassuring squeeze. "It is only the beginning, Olga."

And it was.

She attended the ballet. She ate in restaurants reserved for the party elite and their families. She walked nowhere; taxis were at her beck and call. And, guided by Yuri, she bought presents for her mother in specialty stores that the young girl had never dreamed existed in the Soviet Union.

"All this and more can be yours, Olga, if you learn well."

In her mind Olga agreed completely. No matter what could be asked of her in the years to come, the payment would be minuscule in return for such a lifestyle.

Her talent grew, as did her reputation. Her voice was like no other's, and all who heard it knew that she would be a great star.

What the Russian public did not know was that, beyond her classes, her measured public appearances and her apprenticeship to the Moscow opera, she was receiving other training.

A part of each day was devoted to lectures on the

philosophy of intelligence and the Soviet way of life as opposed to life in the West. Olga studied the philosophy of Marx, Engels, and Lenin as she had never studied it before: how it applied to Soviet intelligence. Almost hourly it was emphasized that the students learn the morality of Soviet intelligence.

"Nothing is immoral. Kidnapping, liquidation, sex, blackmail . . . all are moral acts when done in the service of the state."

Many of the students were shocked. Olga closed her mind to everything but the apartment in Moscow, and graduated at the head of her class.

"Congratulations, Olga Siskova. You have excelled for the good of Mother Russia . . ."

*I have excelled for the good of myself.*

"But this is only the first, and simplest, phase of your training. One day soon you go to Verkhonoye!"

The Verkhonoye School was located about a hundred miles from Kazan, near the Tatar Soviet Republic. It was a desolate area filled with low-lying jagged hills and barren plains. Because of its inaccessibility, Verkhonoye was an ideal location for a spy school that technically didn't exist.

Olga sat silently in the rear of a dark sedan with two other recruits. One was a shy, waiflike girl with large, fearful eyes and an abundance of shimmering black hair. Her name was Larissa Panova, and though she was a year older, she had clung to Olga as a frightened child clings to its mother from the moment she had stepped into the car.

The third occupant of the rear seat had offered no more than his first name: Ivan. He was a slight youth, with darkly handsome features marred only by a slight sneer each time he spoke.

"This is the outer perimeter," their driver growled as the car approached a high, steel-mesh fence topped with barbed wire. "The guard will inspect the identification cards you have been issued."

The guard was armed with a revolver at his belt and a submachine gun slung at his shoulder. He was expressionless as he examined their identification cards one by one. Only once did the icy veneer of his features break. His thin lips curled into an approving leer when his eyes fell on the rounded expanse of Olga's youthful breasts.

Once through the gate, the road wound through low, rocky hills and flat, lifeless prairies. Now and then in the distance an armed guard could be seen accompanied by a leashed dog.

The car came to a halt again at yet a second fence and gate, even more heavily guarded than the first. Again their identification was checked and they were ceremoniously waved through to the inner perimeter.

As the sedan picked up speed, Olga heard Ivan's voice in a thin whisper from the other side of the car. "One must wonder if all of this is to keep others out, or us in."

The living quarters were four barracks broken up by partitioned cubicles. The partitions were made of paper-thin plasterboard, and offered little in the way of privacy.

This didn't bother Olga, even when she realized that the dormitories were to be mixed and the showers communal. Other than the two nights she had spent in the lavish Moscow apartment, she had experienced very little privacy in her life.

"I will not shower with men . . . I couldn't! And to have a strange man sleeping there . . . right *there* . . . it's unbearable! What if, during the night . . . ?"

Larissa's words brought a throaty roar of laughter from

the third member of their cubicle, Tania Paramovna Tupit-syn.

"Ah, little one, a few weeks from now you'll wish all you had to put up with was one young stud's hard cock in the middle of the night!"

Olga winced at the girl's words, but Larissa recoiled in horror.

"What do you mean?"

Tania Paramovna was a tall, raven-haired girl with small but taut breasts and miles of tapering, perfectly proportioned legs. Though she was only twenty, her face had a hardness far beyond her years, and her smoldering dark eyes were as sullen as they were erotic.

Now those eyes studied Larissa's childlike features, and softened slightly.

"Absurd," she murmured. "You really don't know why you're here, do you."

Larissa's face hardened and she stiffened to as much height as her diminutive body would allow. "I am here for the honor of my family and the good of the state!"

"Yes, but to do what?" Tania rasped.

"To learn the gathering of intelligence."

"And you mean to tell me you don't know *how* we are to gather intelligence?"

"I will be told that when the time comes," Larissa replied, her voice cracking slightly under the intensity of Tania's dark-eyed stare.

"Shit," Tania snapped, grabbing a soap dish and a towel and stomping from the cubicle.

Larissa wilted. She fell, rather than sat, on the cot behind her. Her thin, tiny voice was almost a wail when she spoke again.

"Olga, what did she mean?"

"I don't know . . . but I'm sure we'll find out tomorrow."

Olga's class was made up of ten woman and four men. The following morning they were all ushered across the compound to a large glass-and-steel building that housed the school's lecture halls, administrative offices, and laboratory rooms.

"Good morning, and welcome to Verkhonoye. I am Lydya Penkovskaya."

She was a tall, willowy blonde, with striking blue eyes and soft, beautiful features. Only a few tiny lines at the corners of her eyes told the tale of her age. Her figure was youthful, voluptuous, firm, and even dressed as she was, radiated an aura of eroticism and seduction.

Lydya Penkovskaya was dressed in the uniform of a colonel in the KGB.

"You are about to embark on a course of training that will be the most difficult you will ever experience. For some of you, many facets of your training will be distasteful. But you must remember that you are all about to become soldiers in a hard ideological battle. As soldiers you will be asked to do several deeds that might be repulsive. You must consider . . . these deeds are done for the good of your country!"

In the front row, Olga nodded and thought . . . *and myself!*

The welcoming lecture went on for three hours, and consisted of the same propaganda indoctrination that Olga had received at the Marx-Engels School.

During the lunch break, Olga found herself seated next to Ivan. As usual, he was sullen and noncommittal. Except when Olga asked if he knew anything about Lydya Penkovskaya.

"She is a brilliant, ruthless woman who will stop at nothing to see the Soviet Union rule the world.''

Olga nodded. "Then it is that kind of dedication that made her a KGB colonel.''

"Yes. That, and the fact that she fucks well.''

Olga was shocked, but she hid it by withdrawing into herself until she could sort out the meaning of his words.

"Do you mean she has risen in the party by sleeping with her superiors?''

Ivan's chuckle was mirthless. "Not her superiors.''

Olga was angered by his accusation. She toyed with the idea of betraying his derogatory speech to the instructors.

"How is it that you know so much about Lydya Penkovskaya?''

"I should. She is my mother.''

Olga was even more shocked and confused. This time she couldn't suppress exhibiting her feelings, and when Ivan saw her look, he laughed again, louder.

"My mother recruited me to Verkhonoye, because here I can achieve status for her, rather than disgrace.''

"Disgrace . . .''

"Of course. I will excell here. You see, I am a homosexual.''

So then Olga knew. Besides her brilliant talent, they also wanted her body.


Not far from Verkhonoye was the Gaczyna School. It was literally a finishing school for Soviet espionage agents. Few graduates from Verkhonoye were sent to Gaczyna. Verkhonoye graduates were trained to use only their bodies for subversion.

Olga was an exception. Her superiors had looked beyond her exceptional beauty to what they sensed was an underlying core of hardness. She completed her training at Verkhonoye with such detached resolution and fervor that it was suggested she had many more talents than mere guile and seduction.

The Gaczyna School trained the most accomplished assassins in the world.

''At Gaczyna, you will be taught mental and physical discipline far beyond any point you ever dreamed possible. You will become proficient in armed and unarmed combat. You will become adept at melding into the society of any Western country you may be assigned to operate in. And you will be thoroughly indoctrinated with every method known to man in the liquidation of your enemies.''

She learned the credo of Gaczyna: ''Any form of violence must be introduced when other methods of persuasion fail. Adversely, those who would kill must be prepared to die, if necessary, in the interests of our mission and the cause. Here you will be trained to fear nothing . . . not even death itself.''

Olga spent myriad hours poring over the uses of poisons and their antidotes. She became adept at sleight of hand, so a victim would never discern the method used to introduce a narcotic into his body through a drink, a sweet, a cigarette, even a kiss.

She was taught how to repair an automobile, and how to drive it at high speeds through dangerous obstacle courses. Twice a week she parachuted from a low-flying plane until she could spot-jump within inches of a designated target.

One of the most rigorous courses was armament: knives and guns of all types. She learned to use everything from a small-caliber pistol to a single-shot sniper's rifle that could be broken down and concealed under her skirt between her legs. She was taught to fire carefully placed single shots into a man's heart with a .45, or cut a body completely in half with rapid, point-blank fusillades from a submachine gun.

"Always aim at the center of a body. It is a larger target than the head, and has many more kill points."

She mastered highly stylized equipment, such as a silenced gas pistol.

"It has a short range, less than twenty feet, and being less than four inches long, it is easily concealable. It makes barely a sound and kills in four seconds, leaving the cause of death almost impossible to establish."

In six months Olga Siskova was outshooting her instructor.

The full training took a year, and in all that time there was nothing in the curriculum about sex. Olga accepted this as part of the system: turn it on at Verkhonoye and off at Gaczyna, until it was time to turn it on again for the cause.

At last, at the end of a full year, Olga's training was concluded. At eighteen, she was a beautiful and cynical, hard and sophisticated woman who could seduce any heterosexual man at any time. She was capable of giving that man the time of his life, or killing him.

There was only one person who graduated with a higher rank than Olga from the Gaczyna School, the only student besides herself who had gone on to the advanced study from Verkhonoye: Ivan Penkovsky.

After a month's holiday at a resort on the Black Sea, Olga returned to Moscow and her singing career. She had never stopped studying, even with the strain of her intelligence training. In Moscow, she was given yet another complete wardrobe and apartment, and began to work in earnest on her career.

A year later she made her debut, and all of Russia recognized the birth of an operatic superstar. One success came upon another.

For almost two years, she heard nothing at all from the KGB. Then, as if from the woodwork, two of them appeared in her dressing room before a performance.

That evening an English petrochemical engineer would be at the performance. He was an opera buff, and he had expressed a desire to meet the world's next great diva.

His name was Sir Edmund Beals. He would be introduced to her at a party following the performance. Olga's assignment was to seduce him for blackmail purposes.

It took three days for Olga to break down the barriers between them. Then, on the evening of the fourth day, Sir Edmund invited her back to his suite in the Metropole.

He seemed slightly tipsy, but he was more than willing as Olga got him to the bed, undressed him, and then undressed herself.

In minutes they were making love. Olga used every trick she had been taught, every position, every vocal intonation.

Just as Sir Edmund was gasping out the last of his orgasm, Olga's enraged "father" and a friend burst into the room. Olga crawled from beneath the man and began screaming that Sir Edmund had forced her, raped her.

Her KGB "father" and his friend pulled Sir Edmund from the bed and began to pummel him. At the same time, they threatened him with arrest, prison, even death.

Sir Edmund wept. He begged them to stop hitting him, begged Olga to tell them the truth, that it was she who had seduced him.

Sir Edmund was a pathetic, broken figure.

Throughout it all, Olga stood, still nude, her eyes vacant, her face an impassive mask of disinterest.

Suddenly it was over. Sir Edmund stood and, obviously unhurt, pulled on his trousers.

"Marvelous! You have passed your final test, Olga Sis-kova," he said in perfect Russian. "Allow me to introduce myself. I am Aleksei Smislov, Major, KGB. Congratulations!"

"Thank you, comrade," Olga replied, willing the bile to remain in her stomach and her face not to show the anger she felt.

She turned to the two agents. "Did you have to wait until he was through before you broke in?"

The two men shrugged.

"You were wonderful in bed," Major Smislov said with a broad grin.

The three men's laughter followed Olga into the bathroom, where she intended on washing his filth from her body as fast as possible.

In her own words, it was at that very moment when Olga Siskova made up her mind to defect from her Soviet masters the first chance she got.

# FOURTEEN

Carter looked up from the file and out over the veranda rail at a park across the way. It was bright green with fresh spring growth. Buds were still bursting on the trees and birds fluttered about them noisily in their search for the insects that fed on the rich new sap. He could see couples strolling on the grass verges, arm in arm, with all the time in the world and not much to do with it.

Only slightly refreshed, he returned to the dossier. There wasn't much more. A lot of her internal struggle as, for the next seven or so years, she pursued her dual careers.

She detailed her plans for defection, and what she hoped to do after she made it.

Carter finished the file, set it aside, and lit a cigarette.

The sun was starting to set in the park now.

Across the open briefcase and the mound of papers on the coffee table between them, Hawk sat, studying the concentration on Carter's face.

"What do you think?" he said at last.

Carter answered the question with one of his own. "Have you checked it out?"

"The details," Hawk said and shrugged. "That was easy enough."

"And . . . ?"

"It all checks, right down to the names and dates. Of course, her internal strife and her ultimate decisions can't really be checked. They are all in her mind."

"Just what I was thinking." The Killmaster poured a fresh cup of coffee. He sipped it, letting the liquid burn his tongue and activate his brain. "It's one hell of a story, one hell of an admission, and one hell of a denouncement of the Soviet system."

"Exactly," Hawk agreed. "How could this poor woman be anything but what she is after what those monsters put her through?"

Carter turned to the older man and smiled. "But she is."

"I think so."

"So do I," Carter said. "It's too complete, too pat. She says nothing we didn't already know . . . but saying it in public, in a book, bares her soul in the good old American way."

"Exactly," Hawk said. "And there's more. A lot more that wasn't for public consumption."

"Such as?"

"When she defected to our legation in Milan, she was flown directly to Washington for debriefing. The information she provided proved to be a bombshell. Thirteen Russian illegals were rounded up, and nine legals were deported because of it. Remember Ivan and Larissa in her little story?"

"Yeah."

"They were two of the illegals."

"Well, well," Carter chuckled, "that probably put a nice believable cap on it, didn't it?"

"It sure did. It was a coup, and Uncle Sam proved his

gratitude. All kinds of strings were pulled with several coun-
tries so she could continue her career. The rest is history.''

"So if it is just a great big hoax, if Olga Siskova is just
what she was trained to be—''

"She has had twelve lucrative years as one of the best
damn spies ever to come out of Moscow. And, to top it
off, we're going to have one hell of a time proving it.''

"How so?''

"She's revered, Nick, all over the world. My God, she's
practically a bloody goddess in some quarters. Also, she
has enough wealth that it's almost impossible to get to her.''

"So what do you propose?'' Carter asked.

Hawk sat back in his chair. Suddenly the cigar was going
full blast and, around it, the big man's lips had curled into
a leering grin. "I propose we recruit her.''

Carter matched the smile. "You've got a patsy.''

"I sure do. His name is Horst Fender. He's a real hotshot
in the East German government, handles a lot of financial
deals between East and West. He spends most of his time
in Paris and London. He's been working for us about three
years. For two years and six months, we've known he was
a double.''

"How do I play it?'' Carter asked.

"You go as yourself. Convince Siskova that you need
her help. Fender is an opera fanatic. That will make it easier
to get her to reel him in.''

"And then?''

"The Russians don't know we know about Fender. He's
valuable to them. They won't want to lose him if they can
help it. My guess is, she'll set him up for you and then, at
the last minute, go for you instead.''

"Won't she see through that?'' Carter asked.

"She does what she's told. We'll give you a complete
team. You get close to her, Nick, keep the pot boiling.

She'll run to somebody for instructions eventually. When we have the whole net spotted, we pop them . . . all except Siskova herself.''

"And what do you figure from there?"

Hawk mused over this for a moment before he answered. "Nick, that bio you read. What, in her own words, was the running theme?"

Carter thought for a minute and then smiled. "Money, success, prestige, power . . ."

"Right. All the things she couldn't get, even with her talent, in the Soviet Union. All the things she's got here because that's the price the KBG is willing to pay for what she gives them."

"So if she has to run, she won't want to run back to Moscow."

"You've got it. We set it up so that she blows her own net. When she runs, we let her go."

"And let them take it from there. Hawk, you're a treacherous bastard."

"That I am," the big man muttered. "You'll leave in the morning. I've already had our embassy people set her up . . . real cloak-and-dagger stuff."

# FIFTEEN

Carter's juices were up. He didn't wait until morning. He grabbed a nap, packed the new wardrobe supplied to him from the closets of AXE's Paris apartment, and went over the roof to the underground garage in the next building. There he picked up a silver Mercedes coupe and headed south.

By driving through the night with only a few coffee stops, he hit Nice just after dawn. It was a quiet time to arrive in the city. The water was still swirling in the gutters from the nighttime street-cleaning crews, and rubber-booted men in blue coveralls were moving it along with their long brooms.

On the quay, he smelled the scent of roasting coffee from the kitchens, and there was the friendly clatter of chairs being set out on the sidewalks in front of the cafés.

For Carter there was something solid about its simplicity. France would always be France.

It was too early in the morning for the tourists. Even those who were determined to make every second of their vacation count were still sitting in the lounges of their hotels, waiting for the American Express to open, preparing for the day's exhaustions.

For Carter this was good. If anyone took undue notice of his movements, he would also be noticing them.

He drove all the way around the quay and parked in the far end of the horseshoe. Then he casually strolled back to the café called le Court. Two of the outside tables were occupied, one by an old man reading his paper and sipping coffee. At the other table a young American couple pored over a map, sipped café au lait, and kept a wary eye on two enormous backpacks.

Carter took an inside table.

"*Monsieur?*"

"*Un café, s'il vous plaît.*"

"*Oui,*"

It was there in seconds. Carter smoked, sipped, and drank in the sounds and smells around him. Morning bustle merged with the ever-present scent of chocolate. Odd, he mused; nowhere in the south of France could he ever remember the smell of fish, even in the teeming harbor of Marseilles. All the *côte* smelled of chocolate or the sea.

She breezed in ten minutes in front of the appointed time, made right for Carter's table, and bussed him on both cheeks with a wide smile. "*Bonjour, mon cher*. Have you missed me?"

"Like a third hand," Carter replied, rising slightly as she seated herself across the table.

Her name was Latina Cosnolsky. She was Polish, looked Parisian, and spoke better French than most Frenchmen. She had been with AXE for many years. Prior to that, she had toured Eastern Europe as a circus aerialist with her two brothers, Mono and Cathar.

Together they made quite a team.

Her eyes were pale and her hair was fair. She was tallish,

a trifle too thin, and very graceful with a fluid articulation to her limbs. She wore white, and though full summer hadn't yet arrived, her arms and legs were well tanned.

She looked like a schoolgirl on holiday. The appearance was deceiving. Had she not chosen a career as an agent, she would have made a fortune as a cat burglar.

Unlike Carter, Latina ordered an enormous breakfast and, when it came, fell to eating it as though she were a Third World refugee.

"How is the family?" Carter asked.

"Mono is still dying daily of a few hundred assorted diseases. Cathar still can't keep his hands off large-busted young girls."

Carter laughed. Mono Cosnolsky was probably the best electronics man in Europe. The other brother, Cather, was equally adept at visual surveillance. He was also a master of disguise, literally a chameleon who could become anyone.

"Will we see them soon?"

She checked her watch between mouthfuls. "I think they will probably be driving along the coast road around nine."

"And your shopping trip?"

"Complete," Latina said smiling. "Down to the last light bulb."

Carter smiled with satisfaction. All the equipment they would need had been acquired and the two men would meet them somewhere on the *corniche* heading west toward Cannes after nine.

Olga Siskova replaced the dainty bone-china cup in its saucer and turned back to the mirror. She anxiously studied her face as she clipped tiny gold loops to her ears. Not too many lines, thanks to expertly applied makeup. All in all, she was still a damned good-looking woman.

On the outside.

On the inside she was a shell, and it was coming home to her more and more each day. She had even started to watch her food more carefully. The pains were frequent now, almost daily. She knew without seeing a doctor that she had nurtured an ulcer.

She had been at it too long, this dual life. She had gotten everything she had ever dreamed of, even more. She was rich, powerful, still beautiful. But what good would it do her in the years to come?

They would never let her go; never. And in the last year, she had started feeling fear for the first time.

And the previous evening, the phone call. The accent was American, the voice raspy and guttural.

"Mademoiselle Siskova?"

"Yes."

"My name is Dunn. I am with the American State Department."

Her mind whirled and her stomach had erupted until she thought she would faint.

"Mademoiselle Siskova, my people would like to discuss a matter of extreme urgency with you."

"What on earth . . . ?"

"We would like your assistance in a delicate matter. It cannot be discussed over the phone. I wonder if one of our men could join you for luncheon . . . say, tomorrow?"

"Well, I don't know, I . . ."

"It is very important. His name is Carter, Nicholas Carter. He will explain everything. Thank you very much, Mademoiselle Siskova."

Then he had hung up. She had scarcely slept all night, and now, this morning, her eyes showed it.

What, after all these years, could they want? Not since her defection and debriefing so long ago had they contacted her even once. What could they want now?

There wasn't time to alert Sergei Kostovich. She would have to see this Carter person and bluff it out by herself.

Could they suspect her? She had been given far too many assignments in the past year. Too many things could be traced back to her for mere coincidence if the Americans or the British started digging too hard.

"Damn, damn, damn!" she hissed aloud.

*"Pardon?"*

It was Mrs. Kranz. The woman, for all her age and bulk, could enter a room like a cat.

"Nothing. I will be having a guest for lunch. Prepare something light. And, Kranz . . ."

*"Ja?"*

"You may take the rest of the day off once the meal is prepared. I will serve myself."

"As you wish."

The old woman glided casually from the room with the breakfast tray. In the hall, she picked up speed appreciably, heading directly to the quarters over the garage occupied by Alfred the gardener.

Carter handed her into the car and slid under the wheel. Minutes later they were out of Nice and cruising along the coast road west toward Cannes.

He drove slowly, resisting the impulse to get the trip over with as fast as possible. The Mercedes purred. A couple of miles short of Antibes, a dark gray van ran up fast on their rear, blinked its lights, and fell back.

Carter tapped Latina's knee and jerked his thumb toward the rear. She swiveled in the seat, checked, and nodded. "My dear brothers."

Just beyond Antibes, Carter turned off toward the sea. At Juan-les-Pins, he darted into the parking lot of the Hotel Belles Rives. They were already out of the car and walking when the van pulled to a halt several spaces away.

As they passed the van, the rear door opened and the two of them darted inside.

"Welcome to my little bordello on wheels," Cathar Cosnolsky said, grinning and extending his hand. He was tall, several inches over six feet, and with his olive skin, curly dark hair, and perfect white teeth, looked more like a Latin lothario than a Polish defector.

"Cathar, good to see you again," Carter said, shaking the man's hand.

The other brother, Mono, pulled a set of curtains together behind the front seat and also shook Carter's hand.

"Mono, how are you?"

"Not well, my friend. It's my chest again, and I am afraid my eyes are going."

Carter nodded solemnly, glanced at Latina's impish smile, and suppressed a grin of his own.

Where Latina and Cathar were beautiful, their older brother was downright ugly. His body was a foot shorter than Cathar's, and his head was too large for his small shoulders. According to Latina, he had been complaining since birth that he was about to die, but he would probably live to be a hundred.

Cathar opened a bottle of wine, poured four glasses, and they got to work.

From somewhere, the trio had obtained a complete plan of the Château d'Ormanz, the outbuildings, and the surrounding grounds. Latina had already memorized it completely.

"How long will it take you?" Carter asked her.

"I can wire the entire house, the outer buildings, and the cars in two hours if there is no one there."

"Good. Cathar?"

"I have a three-person team at my disposal, complete

with cars and motorbikes. We can track her by car or on foot, every move she makes, day or night.''

''Are they good?''

''The best,'' Cathar replied. ''They could be in her purse and she wouldn't know it.''

Carter turned to Mono. ''You have everything you need?''

The man held his stomach with one hand and gestured to the walls of the van with the other. ''With what I have in here I can hear a cat purr and tell you what it says.''

Carter had carried a manila envelope from the Mercedes. Now he opened it and withdrew two eight-by-ten glossy photographs. He handed them to Cathar. ''Here are the pictures of Horst Fender. How close do you think you can come?''

The tall, dark man studied the photos for a full minute and the sheet attached to the back of one of them with Fender's physical statistics. When he looked back up at Carter he was smiling.

''Past three feet, his own mother couldn't tell us apart.''

''Okay,'' Carter said nodding, ''I'll check in here. The three of you go on into Cannes. Check into the Wagram. It's small and it would fit the budget of three middle-class tourists.''

''When do you see her?'' Latina asked.

''Lunch, today. I won't dump it all on her at once. Until the place is wired and we're set up, I don't want her to move.''

''What's our connection?'' Mono asked.

Carter thought for a moment. ''For meetings, I'll phone for Latina . . . uh, it's a grand day for lunch by the sea. All right?''

''Fine,'' she replied. ''Where?''

''La Coquille. It's in the old town, out of the way.'' Carter stood, or stooped in the van's narrow confines, and moved to the door. "Good luck to us all."

He retrieved his bag and checked into the Belles Rives. The room was small and subdued, but it was over the dining terrace with a beautiful view of the bay.

It took exactly twenty minutes for him to shave, shower, and attire himself as a tourist. This left him fifteen minutes to drive up into the hills and the Château d'Ormanz.

# SIXTEEN

At the same time, in Paris, Carl Rankin sat in a flat overlooking the Bois de Boulogne. In between sips of wine he checked his watch.

The flat was a CIA safe house and it was often used, as it would be used this day, as a meeting place. Carl Rankin was control for an East German agent code-named Spider. Spider was actually Horst Fender.

Promptly at noon, Carl Rankin rose, all five feet three inches and 133 pounds of him, and opened the door in answer to three quick knocks.

Horst Fender, a dark-haired giant beside his control, darted into the room.

"What is going on, Carl? Why the rush?"

"A bit of an emergency, Horst. We have a problem that only someone like you can solve. Very important."

The taller man's eyes narrowed and his face became extremely serious. "Anything I can do, of course."

"You'll have to inform your superiors in the East that you'll be dropping out of sight for a while . . . perhaps as much as a week. Can you handle that?"

"It will be difficult, yes, but I think I can handle it. But why?"

"There is going to be a defection, a top Moscow agent, a woman. She has supposedly been in place for years, and if she is really coming over, she could be extremely valuable to us."

"I see." Fender gripped the backs of his thighs where he sat so he wouldn't let his anxiety show.

"We need to make sure the woman isn't lying. There is always the chance that they may be trying to give her new life by having her confess her past sins, be accepted by us, and play the role of double. After all, Horst, you've been doing the same for us now for years."

"Of course."

Here, Carl Rankin leaned forward and placed his hand on the other man's knee. He bored his beady eyes into Fender's.

"Horst, this is so important to us that we are willing to risk you."

"What?" Fender gasped, color draining from his face.

"Oh, don't worry, my boy. You'll be protected every step of the way. One of our top people is with her now. His name is Nick Carter. He'll be setting you up as her debriefer. We think that, knowing your position, she will be more candid with you."

"But surely that's not enough . . ." Fender sputtered.

"Shh, Horst, calm down. In exchange for our protection, she is giving us the complete list of people in her network, from her control on up and on down."

"That's . . . that's marvelous," Fender said, hoping the sweat wasn't breaking out on his face.

Now Carl Rankin laid it on with a trowel. "Horst, I want the names on that list to be Eyes Only . . . yours. That is, until you can confirm them in the East. I know that you have means over there to do that for us."

"Yes, yes, of course."

"Once the names check out, we will start feeding her information, phony, of course, to feed Moscow. Eventually we will of course pick up the net."

Fender thought for a moment. "But what if the woman isn't really coming over? She will expose me as working for you."

"I told you, Horst, this is worth it. Remember, you'll be protected at all times. You'll leave for Nice tonight. Carter will meet you at the airport."

Both men stood. Fender felt confident now. It oozed in the look he gave the little man and in the way he shook Rankin's hand.

"Accomplish this, Horst, and your retirement in the States is secure."

Fender smiled. *Accomplish this,* he thought, *and I'll be a colonel in the KGB with my own retirement* dacha *on the Black Sea!*

He was all smiles as Rankin showed him out the door. When it was closed and locked, the little man returned to the bar and reached for a brandy bottle.

"Make that two," David Hawk said, entering from the bedroom.

"How did I sound?"

"Perfect, as usual. You should have been an actor, Carl. But did he buy it?"

Rankin bubbled with laughter. "Believe me, Hawk, I can read the man's mind. He was already counting the rubles in his pay raise and sewing the colonel's pips on his uniform tunics!"

# SEVENTEEN

Carter was suitably impressed when he turned off the road into Olga Siskova's estate. Grandeur was not the word.

The sunlight battered the red tile roofs of the huge main house and five large outbuildings. The stucco sides were chalk-white. Palm trees were everywhere, along with lush, meticulously kept lawns.

Carter stopped the Mercedes in a huge cobblestoned courtyard, got out, and approached the door. The tolling of bells inside sounded like high noon at Westminster Abbey.

Olga Siskova herself opened the door. She was impressive in a figure-fitting slack and sweater outfit. Its blue matched her eyes and accented her slender height. The striking blond hair was pulled severely back from her forehead and tied in a tight bun at the nape of her neck.

"Good afternoon, Mademoiselle Siskova. I am Nick Carter."

He flipped his credentials case open and her eyes scanned it briefly. However, Carter had the feeling that she had digested every word and insignia.

In English she said, "Welcome to my house." She held a hand out to him and he brushed his lips across its smoothness. It was ice cold. Her voice was soft and low and very pleasing. Her English was smooth and easy, but touched with a little accent of French and her native Russian. "Come in, please. I have had my cook prepare a luncheon."

She led him through enormous rooms to an intimate, terrace-style dining room. Through the glass lay the shimmering blue Mediterranean five hundred yards below. Carter could see a well-outfitted dock and a sleek yacht.

A twenty-bedroom house on fifty acres of prime Riviera property, a garage full of cars, a pool, stables, and a yacht.

*Lady,* Carter thought, *you've come a long way from a shared one-room flat in Moscow.*

"Please."

She motioned to a small table with only two chairs facing the sea. A large platter of shrimp and oysters, some cheese and bread, a tureen of soup, and two bottles of wine adorned the table.

"I thought it best to give the servants the afternoon off. I will serve."

Carter nodded, keeping his face grave. "I think that was wise."

She flinched a little at that, but covered it well and lifted the top from the tureen.

Conversation during the meal was spotty, bordering on the mundane. She displayed some degree of nervousness but handled it well. Carter felt that she probably handled everything well. He couldn't help but be aware of a certain aura that emanated from her, an aura of calm, composed self-assurance.

He was glad that this composure started to crack a little over coffee and brandy, when the conversation got around to the reason for his visit.

"Just what is your function with the State Department, Mr. Carter?"

He shrugged. "I help people. You might even say that I am a specialist at relocating refugees."

She laughed, a sharp, brittle laugh, and plucked a cigarette from a box at her side.

Carter lit it. "I wouldn't think a woman who lives by her voice would smoke."

"I rarely sing anymore, only a charity recital now and then. But I am sure you know that."

"Of course."

"Come now, let us get to the point. Why, after all these years, am I honored with a visit from the American State Department?"

From his pocket Carter took a photograph. It was a smaller copy of the two pictures he had given Cathar Cosnolsky earlier that day.

"In the past few days, have you seen this man?"

Olga studied the photo. Carter studied her face. He noticed now that there was a puffiness about the eyes. The mouth was full and sensuous, but a little tight with worry lines at the corners.

"No, I don't think I have ever seen that face at all."

"I think you will, very soon."

She glanced up at him. "I don't like games, Mr. Carter. Please get to the point."

She was smoking constantly now, taking deep, quick little puffs that she exhaled abruptly, smoking the unfiltered cigarette to the nub before stubbing it out irritably.

"The man's name is Horst Fender. He is an East German agent, but under direct control of Moscow. Most of the time he operates in the West."

She shrugged and out came another cigarette. "How does that concern me?"

Now Carter chose his words carefully. "It is no secret that we have many funnels for information in both East Berlin and Moscow. A few days ago, we learned that this man, Horst Fender, had been given a special assignment . . . an assignment of assassination."

She didn't blink, but the smoke poured from her mouth and nostrils. "And his target?"

"You, Mademoiselle Siskova."

Again the brittle laugh. "Ridiculous! After all these years, Moscow has washed their hands of me. They would be stupid to resurrect all that now."

Carter nodded and sighed. "At first we thought the same thing. But then we checked, and counterchecked. I'm afraid the order is true, and it came from very high up."

"But why? If anything happened to me, anything violent, the finger would point directly at Moscow."

Carter shook his head. "Not really. You see, Fender has been working for us for some time. We think Moscow may have found out that he is a double. I think, with your past training, you can see what this opens up."

He could see by her features and the piercing sapphire eyes that she was already putting the pieces together. He elaborated anyway.

"As a double, Fender plays a dangerous game. To stay alive and useful to us, he must partially satisfy his Soviet masters. If Moscow saw a way to do away with Fender and you, and blame us at the same time, it would do them far more good than harm."

She was shaken now and didn't bother to hide it. "It's impossible, insane! What am I . . . ?"

"You are a symbol, mademoiselle, a symbol of what life in the West can be for a great talent. Your death, no matter who does it, would be worth a great deal of propaganda."

"Yes," she whispered almost to herself, "it would.

Others would think twice about defecting if they thought that the KGB truly never forgives or forgets.''

"Exactly," Carter replied. "We would like to give you protection, at least until we find this Fender."

She stood and paced, stopping now and then to stare down at the sea. Carter could read the turmoil in her mind, and kept quiet to let it gestate.

Finally she turned to face him. "I will have to think about this."

"I sincerely hope you don't think too long. We have reason to believe that, if Fender hasn't shown up already, he soon will."

"I'll give you an answer by noon tomorrow."

Carter stood. "Fine."

Driving back to Cannes, he knew that the bait in the trap was being nibbled.

And in the big house behind him, Olga Siskova was already making preparations for an emergency meeting with Sergei Kostovich. She couldn't use the usual channels. In an emergency she was to call a florist in Nice and order one dozen red roses sent to Pierre Sautrain in that city. The accompanying card was to read, *Dearest Pierre, why do you never call?*

There was no Pierre Sautrain, but there was a flat in his name in the dock area of Nice. The landlady of the flat would accept the flowers. It was this woman who would contact Major Sergei Kostovich.

# EIGHTEEN

His name was Boris Zaharchenko. He was attached to the Soviet embassy in Paris as the foreign political advisor to the French Communist party. Since the French Communist party had hardly anything to do with real Russian Communists, Boris had much free time for his real job. Colonel-General Boris Zaharchenko was KGB control for over twenty agents in northern Europe, among them Horst Fender.

Now the impatient man was striding up and down, cursing under his breath. Normally on this day of the week, at this time, he would be in Montmartre between the welcoming thighs of his mistress.

Horst Fender's frantic telephone message had ruined his afternoon.

Zaharchenko was short, and stubby, and powerfully built. He had thick black hair, straight and slick. He had a heavy, stolid-looking face with a thick, drooping, old-fashioned mustache, and lively eyes, eyes that were the slightest bit curved up at the sides, as though there were Mongolian blood somewhere but not very much of it.

He looked, at first sight, like a peasant. But there was a sharpness, too, an autocratic arrogance that somehow seemed out of place and unexpected, and the air of competent authority was immense. Peasant or not, the moment Zaharchenko spoke there was evidence of a shrewd and ruthless mind, an ease of manner that denied his origins.

In the old days he would have been killed off as an upstart, destroyed because of a competence that was out of keeping with what would have been called, then, his station. But now, men like these were needed, men whose minds were alert but whose hands were callused, with bitten, grimy nails.

The other man stood watching him. He was tall and slim and cultured, and it seemed that he was trying, successfully, to hide a very real fear. There was a brooding anger in his eyes, but his voice was quiet and controlled, and even polite.

"Comrade Colonel-General, I think it is real. I have a gut feeling that the Americans are actually turning one of ours."

Zaharchenko grunted with derision. "If there were an agent such as they say, I am sure I would know of her!"

Horst Fender bit his tongue to keep from replying to this vodka-sodden peasant who was his superior. He knew that Zaharchenko survived at all only because of his wife's family. Without their intervention the drunken whoremonger would have long ago been recalled to Moscow. As it was, he was given only minor agents to control. Horst Fender was tired of being considered a minor agent, and this was his chance to get away from Zaharchenko.

"If there is such an agent, and a wide network, it may be in our means to save them and stop this woman. It would be a coup for your office, comrade."

The colonel-general stopped his pacing and glared at Fender's tall figure and darkly handsome face. In his mind this man was the new breed, and to Zaharchenko the new breed were all a bunch of ass-kissing incompetent fairies.

But why not? If there was something to all this, he could easily take the credit for it himself.

"All right, Fender. The south of France, you say?"

"Yes, sir. I'm leaving at once."

"Very well. When you have anything, I want you to report back directly to me, no one else. Do you understand?"

"Yes, Comrade-General," Fender replied, suppressing a smile, "directly to you."

Fender beat a hasty retreat and Zaharchenko mulled over the entry he should make in the agents' log that went each day to Moscow Central. He had not gotten where he was by being straight-forward. His strength was in his cunning.

Gingerly, he picked up a pen, drew a message flimsy toward him across the desk, and wrote:

*Spider on special assignment southern France. No contact one week. Believe defection involved agent in place. My office doing extensive research to uncover same.*

There was no need to mention that the Americans had been involved. It would look much better if it was the colonel-general himself who had uncovered this traitor.

Boris Zaharchenko looked up at the clock. With a fast taxi he could still achieve his weekly orgasm.

The adrenaline was pumping through Horst Fender's body as he took the only exit off the highway. He paid no attention to the black Citroën that cut off a car behind him to snuggle against his bumper as he entered the long-term parking area.

He pulled into a vacant slot, grabbed his small bag, and got out of the car. Only then did he realize that the Citroën had pulled up directly behind him.

Two men were getting out of the big car, the driver and a second, bulky man from the rear. They had a look. *That* look.

Fender whirled, meaning to run between the parked cars, and ran directly into a third man. The man was smiling, his arms opened wide as if to embrace Fender. And then he was embracing him, his arms like a vise, locking Fender's arms to his sides.

Fender struggled. He could sense the two men from the Citroën coming up behind him.

He was about to call out, when he felt the sting of a needle in the side of his neck.

At once his legs became rubbery, and seconds later the blue sky over Paris went black.

"He's out."

"Good. Get him in the Citroën. Don't forget the bag."

"I have his keys."

"Take his car back to Paris. Park it on any small street. Lock it and leave the keys in the ashtray."

In less than two minutes, both cars had exited the parking lot and were speeding along the expressway toward Paris.

# NINETEEN

Carter took the night glasses from his eyes, blinked a few times, and again trained them on the hillside on which sat the Château d'Ormanz.

The walkie on the seat beside him crackled, and Mono's voice came over loud and clear. "Nick, someone just opened the other garage door."

"I see it," Carter replied. He watched the old car sneak down the drive without lights. Then the big gates swung open.

"Nick, it's an old woman."

Carter chuckled. "No, it's her. This is probably how she moves around so that no one spots her. Cathar?"

"I'll take her if she goes left, Nick. You take the right."

"Check," Carter said. "Is your man on to the servants in Siskova's Mercedes?"

"Like glue," Cathar answered.

"Latina, are you there?" Carter asked.

"In place," came the woman's voice. "I see her."

"She's yours, Nick," Cathar said. "I'll spell you with my trusty Ford after a mile."

Carter fired up the rented Renault, waited ten seconds from the time Olga Siskova passed by, and fell in behind her.

When Olga Siskova pulled through the gates she noticed the young woman across the street. She snorted. The woman was leaning against the wall, large purse dangling from a long strap at her side, cigarette tilted down from the corner of her mouth.

From her costume and the way she carried her purse, Olga knew that she was a "business girl." Her snort of derision was because, for years, she and her neighbors had tried to have the police keep such women in the downtown area.

The taillights had scarcely disappeared when Latina pushed off from the wall and sauntered across the street. She was halfway to the gates when the van came out of the darkness. It pulled up on the sidewalk and rocked to a halt just in front of the big iron gates.

Latina didn't pause. Like a cat she stepped from the front bumper to the hood and onto the roof of the van. She gripped two of the spikes atop the gate, and her body was a blur as she somersaulted over. By the time she was sliiding down the other side, the van was already gone, joining in on the three-vehicle chase.

By the time they had reached the outskirts of Nice, the van and the two rented cars—Cathar in a Ford Escort and Carter in the Renault—had all traded places three times behind Olga Siskova.

Now Cathar in the Ford was behind her on the promenade, with Carter and Mono running parallel on adjacent streets.

"She's turning north on De Verdun," Cathar exclaimed.

"I'll pick her up at Place Messina," Mono answered.

The radio was silent, and then Mono's voice came up again. "She's going east on the Boulevard Jean Jauris and picking up speed."

Carter quickly consulted the street map of Nice in his right hand, and pushed the Renault up to the fastest speed he dared in traffic. At the Place Garibaldi, he double-parked and barked into the radio, "I'm at Garibaldi."

"Okay," Mono said, "she's heading your way."

A minute later, Carter saw her drive into the square. She took a complete turn at the roundabout, and slowed.

"Get ready," he said, "she's parking . . . she's on foot, Mono."

Across the square Carter saw the van pull into an alley and start its flashers going. Mono appeared and fell in behind the woman.

Carter jammed a cloth cap on his head and put on a pair of heavy-lensed glasses. As he walked, he removed his white jacket, turned it inside out, and pulled it back on. Now he wore a dark blue jacket.

As he passed Siskova's car he saw Cathar already heading that way. Soon he would bend over to tie his shoe. When he stood again, there would be a magnetic beeper under the fender of the car.

They were on the wide Avenue de la République. It was swarming with streetwalkers and neon, loud music and soft entreaties, drifters, pimps, sellers of pornography, Algerians shilling for *"les exhibition,"* and a few honest Frenchmen hurrying to their homes.

The speaker in Carter's ear shaped like a hearing aid, came alive with Mono's voice: "She's stopping at a café."

Carter leaned toward the mike attached to his shirt pocket. "I see."

There was a bistro across the street. He was about to step off the curb, when an oily young man tugged at his sleeve.

"Monsieur . . . you look for company?"

Carter ignored him and moved on. In the bar he took a stool and ordered a cognac. He had a good view of Siskova at one of the sidewalk tables, and Mono at an inside table behind her.

He'd gone through two cognacs and three cigarettes when the woman suddenly stood, threw some money on the table, and took off at a brisk pace.

"Nick . . ."

"Yeah."

"She got a go-ahead sign, probably from someone passing on the street."

"Go, Mono," Carter hissed into the tiny mike. "I'm right behind you."

Cathar piped in. "Need some help?"

"No," Carter said quickly. "We can't afford to have her see you yet. Stay in the car in case she grabs a cab."

He hit the street. Mono was about a block in front, and Siskova a block beyond him.

"*Monsieur?*" It was the oily little man again, sliding along at Carter's elbow.

"*Non.*"

"I have these two fantastic girls, monsieur . . . both eighteen, one French, one Algerian. They stage an amazing performance. You've seen nothing like it. The point, monsieur, is that after it's over, they are both extremely overheated, you would say. And they are prepared to do your bidding. It makes no difference, monsieur—your bidding! The entire program, monsieur, for only two hundred francs."

Carter picked up speed to leave the man behind. He saw Mono suddenly cross the street, and then he saw why.

Olga Siskova had backtracked. She was heading right for him at a fairly brisk pace.

Carter paused until the oily little man caught up with him. He threw his arm around the other's shoulder and moved with him until they were in a doorway.

"Young, you say?"

The man smiled, showing missing teeth. "Babies, monsieur. It's a clean house, very secure, absolutely safe. You won't be disturbed. This French girl, monsieur, you won't find another like her . . ."

Siskova passed without a glance.

"It sounds fascinating," Carter said.

"A bargain, only two hundred francs."

Mono went by. Carter let the man babble on for half a minute, then he abruptly took off.

"*Monsieur!*" the man screeched. "I could make it one hundred and fifty francs!"

"Some other time," Carter growled.

"Monsieur, maybe a boy and two girls? . . . Two boys and a girl . . . ?"

They were back at Place Garibaldi. Carter couldn't see the woman.

"Mono?"

"She has gone into the church of St. Catherine. I'm going in. I'll try to get some shots from the gallery."

Carter made it to the Renault, flopped in the front seat, and lit a cigarette.

She had made a contact. That meant it was going to be a long night.

Within twenty minutes after dropping into the grounds, Latina had bugged all the cars in the garage as well as placing location beepers under a fender of each of them.

The house itself was like a vault, and from the plans she knew that every door and window on the ground floor was wired to an alarm. That was why, like a fly, she had gone up the side of the house and over the roof. Each of the dormer windows in the gables was barred.

She flashed a penlight through each of the windows until she found a room that was obviously empty and unused. When she found one, dusty and bereft of furniture, she spread one of her hands to its widest span, measuring the distance between the bars.

From her bag she took a small lever-jack with rubber buffers at each end. She held the jack horizontally between two bars, fit the handle, and started to crank. It was stiff work, but one of the bars was weaker than the other and it began to bend.

The weaker bar bent until it touched another bar. It was held firm there, and the stronger bar began to bend. Eventually the two bars were far enough apart for her to slip through. Like an eel, she slithered between the bars and tried the window.

*"Merde!"* she hissed under her breath.

Behind the bars, the window was immovable. Obviously it hadn't been opened for years, and couldn't be opened without making a lot of noise.

Latina produced a strong pocket knife and started to cut and pry away the putty around the lower of the two window-panes. Within a few minutes the pane was held in place by only the few small nails that had been under the putty. She put away the knife and brought out some small pliers. Carefully, she extracted all the nails so there would be no chance of tearing her clothes and leaving a clue.

Then she pocketed the pliers and got out the knife again, using it to pry the pane of glass gently forward until it leaned against the window bars. Then she put away the knife. Not once did she put down a tool. After use, every tool was returned to her bag before another was brought out.

Then began the delicate task of slanting and turning the sheet of glass until she had it nearly vertical, at right angles to the windowframe. When this was done, she deftly slid it out between the bars.

Carefully, she set the glass aside and returned to the windows. It was a squeeze, but less than a minute later she was in the house and moving down to the next level.

She started with Siskova's bedroom. Tiny transmitters were planted beneath the bed and the vanity. Then she did a cursory search. As she'd expected, she found nothing.

Then she removed one of the tiny "Cheesebox" bugs from her bag and moved to the telephone. It was only a matter of seconds before the instrument was disassembled. Suddenly, her deft fingers stopped in mid-movement.

"Well, well, well."

Inside the phone was a tiny microtransmitter. Carefully, she pried it up until she could inspect it further.

It was an MS-80, operating on one milliwatt of power with a boost range of only about two hundred yards. The MS-80 was manufactured in a factory in Kiev in the Soviet Union, and it was the favorite telephone bug of the KGB.

Without placing the bug she had brought, Latina put the telephone back together.

She moved on through the house, planting the micro-transmitters, searching, and going over the telephones. She found an MS-80 in every telephone except the one in the cooks's bedroom.

It was clean.

In this one she placed a bug and thoroughly searched the room.

Nothing.

But in the kitchen, in the false back of a bread box, Latina found a three-milliwatt receiver and a mini-tape recorder.

She chuckled. "Spy keeps tabs on spy."

She finished and started back up to the top floor.


"Fender, you say?"

"Yes," Olga replied, keeping her emotions and voice under control. "Horst Fender."

They were in two of the center pews, both kneeling, their heads bowed as though in prayer. Now and then Sergei Kostovich would raise his eyes slightly and frown at her in the pew in front of him.

"But why, Olga, do you want so much information on this man?"

"Never mind. Just get it. I want to know his whereabouts, his current assignment, everything. I also want a photograph, and I want it as soon as possible."

"I will do what I can."

Suddenly she broke every rule by turning to face him and placing her hand on his arm.

"Sergei, do this for me. Perhaps it is nothing. If that is so, I will tell you all about it. We will have a vodka together and laugh."

Again he glanced up, and was shocked. She had tears in her eyes. In all the time he had known her, he had never seen Olga Siskova cry. He didn't know she was even capable of tears.


"Nick, she's on her way out," Mono said.

"I see her," Carter said, sliding down in the seat. "Cathar?"

"Still here."

"Get some shots of him coming out. You and Mono stay on him. I'll take the woman. It's a good bet she's heading home."

"Will do."

Carter waited until Olga was in her car and pulling out before he started the Renault.

The panes were back and the nails returned. A light film of putty had been applied, and Latina was jacking the bars back to their original position, when the receiver in her ear came alive.

"Latina, Nick. She's coming home. We're on the coast road about a mile outside Cannes. I'd say you have about eight minutes. Don't push it. If you're not out, get out."

Feverishly, Latina worked on the last bar. Finally it was close enough. She rammed the jack into the bag and scooted across the roof.

Coming down was much harder than going up. Her weight worked against her rather than acting as a lever for balance. Twice the heavy vines pulled from the house and she hung for several seconds on the verge of crashing into the court-yard. Once she miscalculated the depth of a crevice between the stones, and slipped a good ten feet before catching a vine.

At last she was on the ground and sprinting around the house. As she ran across the vast front lawn, darting among the shrubs and statuary, she could see headlights rising alone along the narrow road from Cannes.

Winded and panting, she dived into a maze of boxwood just inside the gates as the lights rounded the last curve.

Seconds later the gates, controlled by an electronic device in the car, swung open.

She glimpsed Siskova's strained face and then the car was past.

Just as the gates started to close, Latina began to roll.

She just made it, both of them banging her hip as they clanged shut and locked.

In a crouch, she ran along the walk in the shadow of the trees. A hundred yards up the road, around the shelter of the curve, she darted into a cut-out.

The Renault's engine was running. It started moving the instant her butt was in the passenger seat.

Carter glanced over at her. "Okay?"

Latina grinned. "Yeah. And, oh my, have I got some stories for you."

# TWENTY

Carter's weary bones told him that outside it was dawn as Mono Cosnolsky broke open yet another bottle of developing fluid and poured it into the tank.

"How much longer?" he asked.

"This is the last roll," Mono replied, and snapped the white light off, bathing them both in the eerie, darkroom red.

Carefully, he threaded the film from the cartridge onto the developing spool. When the fluid had done its job, he transferred it to a wire and squeezed it dry with a pair of felt tongs.

"How many shots?"

"These are the last six. Cathar took them of the truckdriver at the stop on the Paris highway."

He waved the strip dry and threaded it through the enlarger. One by one, he timed out eight-by-ten prints of the half-dozen shots that had been exposed. He dropped the sheets into the developer and agitated the fluid until images began to appear. When they were legible enough, he dropped them into a stop bath and fixed them.

This done, they ran them through the dryer drum and,

snapping off the red light, got out of the van.

Carter slipped the last six into a manila folder with all the others, and walked across the parking lot to a youth on a motorcycle.

"Pronto," Carter said. "I'd like answers by noon."

The young man nodded, kicked his machine to life, and sailed away.

Carter joined Mono and they entered the hotel. They were halfway across the lobby when Cathar joined them. Together they moved up the stairs in silence.

On the third floor, headed toward Latina's room, Cathar spoke. "The last one, the bakery truck?"

"Yeah?" Carter said.

"There's a squirt transmitter in the rear. I followed him down a little lane off the highway after he made the pickup. I saw the antennae come up out of the roof.

Carter smiled. "Satellite bounce."

"Probably," Cathar replied. "The little lady is in a big hurry."

"She's got reason to be," Mono chuckled.

They entered the room. Latina had used her feminine wiles on the night concierge to rustle up a form of breakfast: hot croissants with butter and marmelade, along with thick black coffee laced with cream and brandy.

They took their time eating and, in silence, watching the resort city get ready for another day. People seemed to come from everywhere . . . workmen, taxi drivers, street cleaners, even a few bikini-clad early risers heading for a good spot on the beach to bake.

They were on their second cups of coffee when the telephone rang.

"*Oui?*" Latina nodded several times, uttered a few "hmmms" and a "yes" or two, and hung up. She turned to Carter. "They are all covered."

"All twelve of them?" he replied.

"The big and the small," she said.

"Okay," he said, rising with a sigh. "We'll see how tense she gets by this afternoon. Cathar, be ready to go tonight if she's ready."

The big man nodded.

Carter headed for the door. "Let's all get some sleep. Call me at my hotel if anything pops before noon."

Latina gave him a look as if to say, "You really don't need to go back to your own hotel . . . ."

Carter avoided it and headed for his car. The invitation was nice, but the body was, unfortunately, weak.

Olga Siskova lay back on the bed, forcing herself to relax. Her eyes were dull and there was a faint smile of derision on her full red lips.

Again she read Kostovich's one-page report and glanced at the photo to which it was attached:

*Subject Horst Fender is one of ours. Works as double out of West Berlin. Current status, on assignment in south of France. Mission unknown.*"

The text was typed. Along the bottom, Sergei had scrawled a message in his own hand: *"Is there some special reason you need this information? I sense a problem. Let me help.*

"Help?" Olga said aloud, and set the message and photo aside. "How can you help, Sergei, when you are part of it!"

Or was he? She couldn't be sure. It could be possible that Sergei knew nothing of Moscow's plans to kill her. That would be like them. The left hand never knew what the right was doing.

She clenched her hands at the back of her neck, so that her thick blond hair rested on the two pillows with which she propped up her head.

It would be difficult, she thought, to give all this up. But something was better than nothing. And *anything* was better than going back to Moscow.

Years before, she had carefully set out to create a third identity for herself. She had built a background, amassed all the papers to prove it, and purchased a home in Recife, Brazil, in that identity's name.

Deep down, she had thought she would never have to use it. Maybe she still wouldn't. Maybe the Americans were just trying to bait her.

For a while she would play the waiting game.

The telephone on her bedside stand rang. *"Oui?"*

"Mademoiselle Siskova, do you recognize my voice?"

"Yes."

"So far, my people have no new developments. But I have been instructed to urge you to accept our offer."

"I am still debating it. It all seems so preposterous . . ."

"It is true, I assure you. And the situation is becoming more dangerous by the hour."

"We shall see."

"Please, mademoiselle, at least allow me to put people around you."

"No, definitely not."

She hung up. For a full moment she stared at the phone, biting her lip. Then, on impulse, she got a number from the directory and dialed.

*"Bonjour*, my name is Marie. Thank you for calling Air France. How may I help you?"

"I would like flight availability from Paris to Buenos Aires, please."

"First class or coach?"

Olga smiled. "First class."

In the kitchen, Mrs. Kranz waited until the tape stopped. Then she wound it and played it back. She scowled as she listened to the recording. When it finished, she replaced the false back in the bread box and hurried to her quarters and her own phone.

Carter replaced the telephone and ran his eyes down the scrawled list he had just completed.

The net handling Olga Siskova had grown to fourteen. A team from Paris was already on the scene. They could be picked up in seconds.

After it had been learned that the cook and the chauffeur/gardener were KGB watchers and backups, a second team had been assigned to them. But the cook and the gardener would escape, slip through the net. That was an integral part of the plan.

It would be quite a haul, Carter mused, quite a haul indeed.

Again he reached for the phone. It was time to go into Cannes for lunch.

The Killmaster was finishing his second cup of coffee when Latina, looking every inch the tourist in pink stretch slacks and a loose overblouse with a scoop neck—a very scoop neck—slid into the booth.

"All kinds of goodies," she said once the waiter had deposited coffee and left. "La Siskova checked out Paris-to-Buenos Aires flights. Mono caught it when the cook used her phone to report."

"Did she make reservations?" Carter asked.

"No, but she got flight times for the next three days."

Carter nodded. "Then she needs just one more little push. Tell Cathar we go tonight."

Sergei Kostovich was worried. He had worked too long with Olga Siskova. He knew her quirks and her moods. Olga was not a nervous woman and she did nothing without a good reason.

In the past twenty-four hours, she had exercised

emergency procedures twice. Unheard of. And, to make matters worse, she had given him no clear reason.

Now Olenin had flown in from Rome and summoned him to a meeting in the Nice safe house. "A matter of grave importance," he had said, and he had made direct contact.

Kostovich rang the bell and through the glass saw the old woman approach down the dim hall to open the door.

"I am Monsieur Martine."

The woman nodded. "Top of the stairs, first door on the right. He is waiting."

The door had scarcely closed behind Kostovich when two men emerged from a shadowed doorway across the street. From a car a block away, two more hefty types in dark jackets emerged and walked toward the house. In the rear, a team of three men were already picking the lock on the alley door.

Eight miles away, Jules Piseur emerged from a roadside café and walked toward his paneled delivery truck. He was almost there when two men emerged from the shadows to block his way.

"Jules Piseur?"

"*Oui.*"

One of them opened a small leather wallet and held it in front of Piseur's eyes.

"André Hubert, S.D.E.C.E. You are under arrest, Monsieur Piseur."

"Me? *Mon Dieu,* for what does the security police want me?"

"For operating as the agent of a foreign government."

All over the Côte d'Azur that night, similar arrests were being made.

# TWENTY-ONE

Clouds covered the moon like a gray blanket. Even if they hadn't, it would have been impossible to see the dark-clad figure dart from tree to tree and shrub to shrub until the man was at the side door of the garage.

Silently, he opened the door and slipped inside. A light was on in the apartment above. Like a cat, he went up the stairs.

The man and woman sat at a table, facing each other over a bottle of schnapps. At the last second they heard the slight creak of a hinge as the door opened.

It was not warning enough.

The gardener, Alfred, leaped up, but a blow to the side of his neck felled him like a tree. The woman started to scream, but all sound was cut off by iron fingers at the side of her throat.

The man worked with speed and deftness. He cut pull cords from the drapes to bind them, and then gagged them with socks from the man's dresser.

The man, Alfred, was out cold. The woman stared from the floor, wide-eyed, at the intruder as he crossed to the telephone. He placed his body between the phone and the woman's eyes. He dialed, but before the phone rang he cut the call off with a finger.

"The servants are secure. Is she ready to go? . . . Good, I'll be waiting at the gate."

He replaced the instrument and, with one last look at the bound couple, moved down the stairs. From the first car he took the electronic device that opened the front gates. Outside, keeping in the shadows, he darted to a prearranged spot at the wall surrounding the estate.

"Nick?"

"Here," came the reply from the other side of the wall.

Cathar Cosnolsky lofted the device over the wall and took off at a dead run for the house.

Olga Siskova stepped from the tub and patted herself dry with a huge towel. When her body was powdered and perfumed, she wrapped a smaller towel around her damp hair and moved into her bedroom.

A sheer negligee was just whispering down over her body when a sound in the hall outside her door made her turn.

"Kranz?"

The name had scarcely escaped her lips when the door burst inward. Through it came a man dressed all in black. Olga instantly recognized the face, and leaped over the bed, clawing at a drawer in her bedside stand where she always kept the loaded Beretta.

Carter waited until the noise from the bedroom resembled World War III, and then bolted into the room.

It was a shambles.

Olga Siskova, fighting in silent ferocity, was pinned to the chaise longue by Cathar. The savagery of her struggle was evidenced by the overturned furniture, the broken vanity mirror, and the scattered jars of cosmetics strewn over the floor.

The couple's heavy breathing filled the room as Cathar's powerful hands folded around the woman's throat. Warding off her clawing fingers at his eyes, and avoiding the thrashing of her legs, he began to apply pressure, making her gag and gasp for air.

Carter suppressed a smile. Poor Cathar. She was giving him all he could handle.

Even as he thought this, Siskova managed to slam the heel of her hand against Cathar's nose. His blood spurted and she was momentarily free.

Cathar growled in fury. He grasped the woman's hair and pinioned her head against the cushion. In desperation Siskova rolled from the chaise, pulling him with her. Cathar grasped her again by the throat, slammed her head against the floor, and sprawled heavily over her body.

*That,* Carter thought, *should do it.*

Unseen by the struggling man and woman, Carter glided across the floor. Grasping Cathar by an ankle, he swung the big man aside by the leg. Cathar skidded along the carpet, plowing through the debris to crash against the wall. He rolled to his back, a Makarov automatic in his hand.

Carter's own right hand darted under his jacket. Wilhelmina bucked once, the sound a mere hiss through the silencer.

The center of Cathar's chest blossomed crimson. The gun dropped from his hand. He managed to come up on one knee, and then pitched forward onto his face.

Carter turned to the woman. She lifted herself to a sitting position, staring in hatred at the fallen man, ignoring her own nakedness. Only a few shreds of her negligee remained.

Most of it had been ripped from her body. Her throat and breasts were still flushed with the red bruises inflicted by Cathar's hands.

Suddenly she leaped up, in a flash of ivory legs, and scooped up a broken jar. Carter grasped her hands, preventing her from grinding the glass into Cathar's neck. She struggled, and Carter was conscious of the animal scent of her.

"Dammit, there's no time for that now!" he hissed.

With a last squeal of anger, she dropped the jar. "Bastards! They're all bastards!"

"I was tailing, but he gave me the slip. When he did, I headed right here. You were set up, Olga. You have been for a long time."

"What do you mean?"

Carter grabbed the phone from the floor and ripped it apart. "See this? If you don't know, it's an MS-80."

Her blue eyes blazed. "KGB."

"You'd better believe it. C'mon."

He tugged her to the kitchen and pulled the bread box apart to reveal the tape recorder.

"Kranz!" she spat.

"You've probably been under surveillance since the day you defected. It was just a waiting game until the time was right."

He kept the pressure on. He knew she had taken it all. Now it was just a matter of playing out the string.

Taking her by the hand, he tugged her back up the stairs. He yanked a blanket from the bed and covered Cathar's "corpse."

"Get dressed. Pack a small bag, just your jewels and a few clothes."

"What are you going to do?"

"Take you to Paris. I can hide you there until we can

smuggle you out of France and into England. It will take a few months, but eventually we can get this all straightened out and you can have your life back. After fouling up this attempt, I don't think they would dare try again.''

Her whole attitude changed, just as Carter was sure it would. ''Yes, Paris,'' she murmured. ''That's an excellent idea.''

Twenty minutes later Carter handed her into the Mercedes and drove through the gates, leaving them open behind them.

The Mercedes had barely passed out of sight when Mono and Latina darted up the drive and into the house. In the bedroom, Latina yanked the blanket from Cathar.

''Wake up, Sleeping Beauty.''

Cathar stood, smiling even though his face was a mass of scratches. ''It went well.''

Latina chuckled. ''You look like hell.''

He shrugged. ''The bitch was a wildcat.''

''Hurry,'' Mono said. ''We must clean this up. There must be no trace that the woman didn't just peacefully disappear.''

The night was warm. The traffic on the highway north was light. The clouds were clearing away now, revealing a new moon.

Wind blowing through the open windows of the car tousled her blond hair as she sat in the passenger seat. The changing amber and white of passing lights flickered across her stern, immobile features.

In the last two hours, Carter thought, that face had been transformed. Oddly, it was no longer beautiful. All the hatred and bitterness of the betrayal she thought about was mirrored in her face.

He lit a cigarette and returned his eyes to the road. She would dig her own grave now. He had no doubt of it.

• • •

Horst Fender hurried along the Rue Diane. His steps were still a little wobbly and his eyes were still not focusing very well.

He could make no sense out of anything. An hour earlier, he had awakened on the Paris Metro. One glance at a newspaper and he knew that he had lost three days of his life. It was surreal, impossible. But, somehow, it had happened.

Now it was almost dawn and he felt weak, too weak to report in. He had decided to return to his flat. There, he would put it all together before reporting in and possibly putting his neck in a noose.

His hand was shaking so hard he could scarcely get his key in the door.

They were waiting, two of them. Their faces and their clothes told him who they were.

They were not gentle. Without a word, one of them slammed Fender against the wall and bent his arms painfully up between his shoulder blades. The other one went through his pockets.

"Were you thinking of taking a trip, Comrade Fender? For your health, perhaps?"

"What?"

The man waved an airline ticket in Fender's face. It was for an Air France flight to Buenos Aires that morning. The ticket was made out in his name.

Attached to it was a folded slip of paper. It was scented.

"What does this mean, Comrade Fender: 'Do not speak to me on the plane. As per our agreement, I will meet you at the Café Penguin on Avenida Asencion in two days' time, noon. There we will conclude the terms of our agreement.' What agreement is that, comrade?"

Fender fought desperately to clear the cobwebs from his

brain. "I don't know. I don't know anything about this. I swear . . ."

"And this list of names, comrade. What does it mean?"

"I don't . . ."

The man's fist slammed into the side of Fender's head.

The next thing he realized, he was being dragged down the stairs between the two men.

# TWENTY-TWO

There was a concierge's apartment on the ground floor of the building. Carter rapped on the glass window that framed the upper half of the front door. Through a patch of lace he saw an old man come down the hall in his robe and slippers. In a moment the door opened.

"I believe you have a room for my wife and me. The name is Carter."

"*Oui*. Come in out of the rain." They stepped into the foyer and shook the rain from their shoulders. "Spring in Paris," the old man chuckled, "always the sudden storm. This way."

He led them up two flights of stairs and down a dimly lit hall. He opened a door and snapped on a light.

"The room, of course, has been prepaid."

"*Merci*," Carter replied.

The old man shuffled away and Carter shut the door.

"You'll be safe here until I can make some arrangements."

"You're leaving?"

He nodded. "I should be gone only a few hours. Get some rest."

He was headed for the door when Olga's voice stopped him. "Carter . . ."

"Yes?"

"Have you ever heard me sing?"

She had seemed dead on the drive. Now her eyes were alive again, piercing, as they had been on their first meeting. For the first time, Carter realized her age. There was a strain in her handsome face and a rigidity in her athletic body.

"Yes," he replied, "once. Several years ago, in Milan. It was *Lucia di Lammermoor*."

Suddenly she laughed. "My greatest role. Tragedy becomes me."

For a brief second, Carter thought she would lean forward and kiss him. Instead, the light in her eyes drained away and she turned toward the bed and her bag.

He almost felt sorry for her. But then he remembered the old woman's face and the bullet-stitched body of the old man in the rear of the Cherokee.

"I always thought Lucia was a flawed opera."

"Oh?"

"Yes. Lucia dies offstage."

Carter bounded down the stairs and, turning the collar of his coat up to ward off the rain, ran for the Mercedes. He drove five blocks away, parked on a small side street, and retraced the route on foot.

Horst Fender sat, exhausted, in the chair across from Colonel-General Boris Zaharchenko. His body was bathed in sweat and every inch of it ached. They had beaten him with damp, rolled-up magazines. That would be so there would be no visible bruises when they put him on the Aeroflot flight for Moscow.

They hadn't told him that was what they were going to do, but he knew that was the case. He had seen it done with too many others.

Boris Zaharchenko was roaring, his face above his wilted collar beet red.

"Every one of them, every man and woman on this list, is now under arrest by French security!"

"Comrade Colonel-General . . ." Fender whined.

"And you still deny that you passed these names to the Americans?"

"I didn't, I swear!"

Zaharchenko snorted. "You are the worst kind of traitor, Fender. Do you still deny that you have conspired with Siskova, become her tool?"

"I never reached the woman . . ."

"You lie, Fender!" the old Russian roared. "You helped her escape! Bring in the man and woman."

The door opened, and a plump woman in her fifties and a tall, gaunt man of about the same age entered.

"Frau Kranz . . ."

"Yes, Comrade Colonel-General?"

"Is this the man who attacked and bound you?"

"Yes, Comrade Colonel, I am sure of it."

"And you?" Zaharchenko said to the man.

"There is no doubt of it, Comrade Colonel-General."

Fender tried to rise from the chair. "I swear, I have never . . ."

"Silence! Take him away!" When the couple left and Fender had been dragged from the room, Zaharchenko turned to his aide. "Everything is prepared at the airport?"

"Yes, Comrade Colonel-General. We are watching every flight."

The hall was empty, the old hotel quiet, when Olga Sis-

kova, in her gray wig and cast-off clothes, emerged from
the room. She located the rear stairs and went down them
without a sound.

It was clear sailing, and within minutes she was in the
rain-soaked alley. She held her pace, steady and slow, as
would a woman of her advanced years. At the mouth of the
alley she turned right, toward a larger boulevard where she
could locate a taxi.

A block away, in a dry doorway, Carter flattened against
the door, his body in shadows, the doorway itself washed
by the sheets of rain.

He watched Siskova cross the street and step into a taxi.
When it pulled away, he walked leisurely to the Mercedes.

There was no hurry. He knew where she was going.


"Your passport, please."

Olga Siskova handed the woman her passport and smiled
sweetly. The photo was checked, a tag was put on her single
bag, and the passport and ticket were handed back.

"The flight will be boarding in a half hour, Madame
Bonez. Gate Seven."

"Thank you, thank you very much."

"Have a nice flight."

She was halfway across the concourse when she saw
them, a man and a woman. There was no mistaking the
clothes, the look. She had seen the type hundreds of times.
She had grown up with it.

They were heading straight for her, their faces grim.

She changed direction.

Two more, a man and a woman, clones of the first pair.
They were hemming her in, moving her.

She turned as if to backtrack, only to find that there were
four of them fanned out behind her, boxing her in.

They wouldn't dare, she thought, not in broad daylight in a crowded airport.

They wouldn't dare.

Would they?

Between two pillars on a walkway high above Air France's grand concourse, Nick Carter stood, his hair matted wildly to his head, his hands deep in the pockets of his tan trench coat.

A cigarette in the corner of his mouth curled smoke up to mask his hooded eyes as he watched the drama unfolding below.

It was done perfectly, as if every move had been choreographed.

That thought brought a smile to his lips.

*Just like an opera.*

They enclosed her as if their bodies were a funnel through which she passed. Short of breaking into a run and charging right through them, she had no choice.

At the last second before the first team reached her, she darted into the only avenue of escape left to her, a ladies' room.

The door was still closing when an old woman in a gray uniform and a soiled apron came around the corner. The sea of dark-suited men and husky, tweed-skirted women parted, and the old woman darted through with her cart piled high with linens.

Without a pause she hung a sign saying Out of Order on the door, and pushed the cart inside. Two of the husky women followed her, one of them already fumbling in her purse.

Carter lit a fresh cigarette from the butt in his lips.

His imagination could picture the offstage scene.

Surprise. A brief struggle. A quick jab with a hypodermic needle. Half of the linens would have already been lifted from the cart.

Her weight would be nothing for the two husky women. The linens would be replaced.

Carter checked his watch again.

"Now," he whispered.

The cart reappeared.

Two minutes to the second had elapsed.

He rode the escalator down to the main floor and followed along, just keeping the cart in sight. They went through the huge Pan Am concourse and along a riding escalator to the boarding areas of four other airlines.

When he saw the woman pause in front of an elevator, he himself stopped. Stamped across the doors of the elevator, in large red letters, were the words STAFF ONLY. When the doors closed behind the woman and the cart, he turned and mounted another escalator to the obervation platform above.

At the top of the escalator, he scanned the arrow signs until he spotted the one he wanted: AEROFLOT.

At a nearby bar, he ordered a brandy. When it came, he walked to one of the huge windows and settled back on one of the vinyl-covered lounges.

Below him, a huge white-and-blue Aeroflot jet was being loaded: passengers to the right side of the plane, freight and baggage to the left. Casually, he sipped the brandy, watching the long line of baggage go up the twin conveyor belts into the gaping hole in the side of the jet.

Then he saw a catering truck back up to the door of the rear galley. Between the rear of the truck and the plane, there was only a seven- or eight-inch space. But it was enough.

He saw two in-flight stewards, the blue, encircled *A* shining on their caps, dart past the opening. Both of them had their arms around a tall woman in a cloth coat.

Above the turned-up collar of the coat, he saw a flash of the gray wig.

It was another fifteen minutes before the cargo doors were closed and sealed, and the passenger jetway motored away from the plane. When the two hatches on the left side were secured, the plane began to roll. When the tow wagon had pushed the big jet completely clear of other planes on either side and the building, it was disconnected and the jet's engines roared. By the time Carter had finished the brandy, it had reached its takeoff position at the end of the runway.

He stood and walked toward the escalator. On the main floor, he found a telephone.

"Yes?" the voice said after the first ring.

"This is N3," Carter replied. "The vodka has been picked up."

"I'll inform Mr. Pause."

Carter walked from the terminal into the rain. Halfway to the van, he heard the roar of a jet taking off. He looked up.

For a few seconds he watched the big white jet as it curled toward the general direction of Moscow.

"How did it go?" Latina asked, as Carter climbed into the van.

"According to the script," Carter replied. "Lucia died offstage."

# DON'T MISS THE NEXT NEW
# NICK CARTER SPY THRILLER

## *INVITATION TO DEATH*

The truck was behind one of the cottages under a crumbling lean-to. It looked in decent shape with fair tires.

Carter darted a quick look around, then began to slither across the open area. But he never made it. A tall man in a fur coat and hat stepped around the corner of the cottage and leveled an automatic at him.

"Good afternoon, Carter. My name is Orlov. Please cooperate. My orders are to take the documents from you and let you and your group proceed on your way."

Carter moved his hands out from his sides. "I am not armed."

"That is good. Bodies are so messy. The documents, please."

"Orlov, is it?"

"Yes."

"I don't have the film, Orlov."

"Please, please . . ."

"But I do have Major Arksanova."

The surprise on his face was genuine. This new development made his concentration stray just enough.

Carter jumped, got hold of the gun, and held on. It fired wildly. The Killmaster butted Orlov with his head, catching him on the chin. Orlov went down, the gun flying into the snow.

Carter rushed him, swung an intentional wild right, and jerked back as Orlov tried to block it. He was open in the stomach. Carter hit him as hard as he could. Orlov bent over and landed in the snow, then sprang back up, lunging at Carter. They went down together.

The Russian had Carter around the throat, riding him with his weight and forcing his face into the snow. No matter what the Killmaster tried, he couldn't free himself and he was having trouble breathing.

Suddenly the weight was gone. Carter rolled to his knees.

Orlov was staggering to his feet. Beside him, Lola stood, a huge hunk of shattered wood in her hands. As Orlov moved, she laid it across his back again, and it shattered completely.

"We spotted him," she said. "I followed you."

"I can see. Where are his friends?"

"Guarding the road on the downside of the village . . ."

Orlov came off the ground like a roaring bull to plant his shoulder in Lola's belly. She sailed, and the Russian scrambled in the snow for his gun.

It was obvious to Carter now that Orlov assumed he was bluffing about his superior's wife. Carter ran at him and kicked him in the face. Orlov went down and Carter kicked him again.

The Russian turned and tried to crawl away, but Carter ran alongside him, kicking him like a dog.

Orlov jumped up suddenly, and lunged, managing to get

his thumbs into Carter's throat.

The Killmaster jabbed both hands into the other man's eyes, pushing with all his strength. Orlov released his grip, and Carter tore free. At the same time, he lashed the Russian in the face, jumped behind him, and locked his arms, lacing his fingers in back of the other's neck.

It was the end.

"Quit, Orlov," Carter hissed.

The Russian struggled, kicking backward with his right leg.

Carter tightened his hold. Orlov stomped the ground and tried to throw Carter off his back. The Killmaster hung on, applying pressure. More and more pressure. He pulled back hard, straightening his arms with the last of his strength.

Orlov's neck snapped.

His head fell forward loosely on his chest and he sagged to the snow. His body quivered, his right leg twitched several times, and then he lay still.

Carter sank to the ground, his breath coming in short, desperate gasps. Lola's feet appeared at his side.

"You're all right, aren't you?"

"Oh, hell, yes," Carter wheezed. "I'm Superman. See if the keys are in that damn truck."

He staggered to his feet and moved after her. Just as they reached the truck, an old man emerged from the rear door of the cottage.

"The keys are in the ignition," Lola said.

"Is this your truck, old man?" Carter said. The man nodded. "We're buying it," he said, and turned to Lola. "Pay him."

"With my money?" she squeaked.

"You bitch . . ."

"All right, all right," she said, leaning out the opposite window and shoving a wad of bills into the old man's hand.

Carter started the truck and backed from the lean-to in a swirl of snow.

The truck was behind the cathedral. Tommaso was in the driver's seat revving the engine. Lola sat beside him. Arturo and Regis Caylin were in the rear, behind the sideboards.

Gabin Fullmer was helping Carter lash Major Bella Arksanova across the grille. With each tightening knot to her wrists and ankles, she spouted a new stream of curses at them in Russian.

"Do you think this will work?"

"If it doesn't, she gets it first," Carter replied. "And my guess is they won't want to answer to her husband for that."

"That does it," Fullmer grunted, tightening the final knot.

"Okay," Carter said, "you get in the back. Those of you with guns, don't use them unless they fire first and we have to shoot our way through." He climbed into the truck. "Tommaso . . ."

"*Si?*"

"Go slow, very slow. If they don't move the barricade, I tell you when to crash it."

"*Si.*"

The truck rolled slowly forward.

The tension was so thick it would have required a machete to cut through it.

They couldn't see the KGB agents, but they could spot the snouts of their guns poking from behind trees and over fallen logs.

Tommaso inched the truck forward in its lowest gear. About four hundred yards from the makeshift barricade across the road, one of them fired a warning shot.

"Don't stop," Carter said. "Just keep going slow. They'll recognize her soon."

"*Sì.*"

"Maybe they won't give a damn," Lola said, her voice quivering.

Carter shrugged.

At two hundred yards, they recognized the parka-clad woman draped across the front of the truck. There were shouts back and forth across the road, and one man stood full up to make sure.

"Keep going," Carter said.

At twenty yards from the barricade, Bella Arksanova broke. She started screaming in Russian at the men in the trees. Two of them dropped their rifles and ran into the road waving their arms.

"Stop," Carter said, a sigh of relief in his voice.

Tommaso braked the truck and calmly lit a small cigar.

It took the men fifteen minutes to remove the logs and debris from the road. When they were finished, Tommaso eased the truck through. Five pairs of hate-filled eyes watched their progress.

"Hit it!" Carter hissed.

They careened down the mountain for nearly five miles as fast as the truck would go.

Bella was shouting at the top of her lungs.

Carter leaned out the window. "What did you say?"

"I am freezing! You are freezing me to death!"

"Won't be long now."

He rolled up the window and lit a cigarette.

Five miles later he called a halt and cut her loose. "Strip."

"What?"

"Strip, comrade, down to your shoes."

"I will freeze!"

Carter shook his head. "No, you won't. It's warming down here and the snow has turned to rain. Strip!"

She did, finding new curses for him with each item. When she was stark naked, wearing only her shoes, she started to weep.

"Don't cry, Major," Carter growled. "Just start back up the road. Your friends will catch up with you."

He crawled back into the truck.

"Let's go. Head for Zaragoza!"

—From INVITATION TO DEATH
A New Nick Carter Spy Thriller
From Jove in February 1989